I0717016

BREACHED

LAWRENCE J. WEST

There is a truth that lurks within all civilization:
Death is patient. Life is forgetful.

*Trigger Warnings for homophobia, xenophobia, dismemberment, gore, death, extreme violence, and death. If you'd like more detailed information on the content, please do not hesitate to reach out to us at contact@inkedingray.com

CANDACE

Final transmission. Sent 5:34 PM

Zurathel Transit Outpost 9106
Location: Planet 802.17 (3rd Galaxy, inner ring. Uninhabitable.)
Crew: 65 (Human)
Gate Classification: Dual Relay. Net Accessible. Clip Operated
Commander: Candace Pruit
Second in Command: Science Officer Travis Scanlon

There is a truth that lurks within the heart of all civilization. Death is patient. Life is forgetful.

Candace Pruit reclined in her chair and propped up her feet on the rarely-used control panel. Alone in the control room she spoke with her wife's projection via her clip, a thin metal disc implanted halfway down the back of her neck, while she waited for the last gate alignment of her tour to start. A cold drink called to her as the last of her patience faded.

"Shit, Julia. I'm done talking about this," Candace said for the hundredth time. "Yelling at me isn't going to make time move any faster, and it's not going to erase the past three years. I did this for us."

The image of Julia sat firmly in the center of Candace's vision, projected onto her mind. The image window was a small piece of what the neural link technology did, but it was a welcome one for those like Candace who sometimes spent years away from their partners and families.

A chime rang in her ears and a message popped up in the lower part of her vision, partly obscuring the image of her wife.

Official Notice
From: Tsoral Nievel, Director of Operations
To: All Outpost Commanders

Subject: Gate Recalibrations

This is a reminder to all crews located at gate outposts that they may experience fluctuations in gate readings. These are expected as the overflow system recalibrates. Please disregard these anomalies unless they become persistent and exceed the levels specified in previous briefings.

"Shut up," Candace said, swiping the memo away with a flick of her fingers. In an hour she would be done with this job and would have no more use for the hail of memos and reminders that came down the chain of command. Her priority was assuring her wife that —

"It's just hard here," Julie said. "I still don't know why I couldn't come along like I did when you were stationed at Santalaria." She pouted. Her eyes were red and puffy, contrasting her blonde hair and makeup that still looked perfect.

The sight of her wife so distraught thawed Candace's frustration. Candace would make it up to her. The house she bought for them would be a start. She envisioned the joy on Julia's face when she saw it for the first time. Happy tears would replace the ones that now silently spilled down her wife's cheeks.

Candace groaned and shut her eyes, but the virtual heads up

display was still there behind her eyelids. As marvelous as the clip was, there was no hiding from what it showed.

The calendar app pinged and the numbers in the top left of her vision flashed red. Candace glanced up, bringing the clock to the center and forcing the window with her wife to move right. Fifteen more minutes till the Avealus Gate aligned and last guests arrived. Retirement was almost here.

"I already told you. They don't allow spouses to come along to outposts like this. There's no shopping. No sightseeing on my days off. Trust me, you didn't want to be locked in this box for three years. It was hard enough to keep the workers from going stir crazy, let alone their families. That's why they paid me so much to take the post. No one else would do it."

Julia scowled and said nothing. Candace's clip pinged again.

"Listen Julia. I have to go and prep the gate. I got the last group coming through, but I'll call when my shift is done. Okay? I love you."

Julia pursed her lips, her face stony and red. "Fine," she said, and the window blinked out.

A robotic female voice spoke through the speakers. "Fifteen minutes until gate alignment."

The chair creaked as Candace pushed further back to study the familiar gray brick of the ceiling. After nearly twenty-five years of running outposts like this all over the galaxy, it was strange to be seeing them for maybe the last time. At least as an employee. Odds were, if she and Julia did any traveling, they would end up at one of the eleven thousand outposts. But a brief visit would be better than a long stay.

The clock showed that she had fourteen minutes left until the Avealus Gate on Outpost 9106 and the one on Vexel-7 would be aligned. The computer's voice intoned this.

Candace dropped her feet and sat up before straightening her uniform. Robotically she flipped two switches. The solid steel shield that separated the control room and the hangar lifted, illuminating the enormous room that contained the ancient structure. It was protocol to leave it shut when the gate was not in alignment, and while no one would have cared or even known that she left it open, it was better to lead by example and show her crew that policy and procedure mattered.

The hangar was half a mile long and three quarters of a mile high. It was barren except for two doors — one leading to a waiting area and the other leading into the outpost. The stone archway of the Gate stood against the far wall more than a thousand feet away.

Candace gasped. The Avealus Gate was not illuminated as it should have been. Instead, a flat dead blackness resided within the confines of the stone. The hair on her arms stood on end as she stared at it. Was something wrong? Should I do something? Say something? The warning bells in her mind chimed loudly but then she thought of Julia, of seeing her wife, of freedom. It was probably nothing. Just a little variance. If something was actually wrong, the system would tell her. She checked the readings on her clip anyways and they didn't show that anything was out of the ordinary. Yet something —

"Creepy, isn't it?" asked a voice from behind her.

Candace jumped and whipped around as her replacement doubled over with laughter. She gripped her chest, digging her fingers deep into the flesh over her heart and waited patiently for her breath to return to normal while Jackson held himself against the doorframe, grubby in his faded jeans and blue t-shirt. Like everyone else at this outpost, he didn't bother wearing the company uniform. Only Candace bothered. Her white shirt bore her name and the corporate insignia. Her black slacks were perfectly pressed. Who else was going to set the example if not the person in charge?

"What the fuck?" Candace yelled. "You trying to kill me?"

"Sorry," Jackson said between laughs.

"What the hell are you doing here anyway? I gave everyone the night off. Including you. Go enjoy it." Candace made no attempt to hide the contemptuous dismissal from her voice.

Jackson frowned. "Yeah, well, my promotion starts for real in fifteen minutes, and I figured it couldn't hurt to have you walk me through the gate alignment procedure one more time. It's all on me after you leave and it should at least appear like I know what's going on."

Candace scowled. *Fat fucking chance of that happening. The Zurathel Transit Corp must be desperate if they are promoting a dipshit like Jackson.*

"Thirteen minutes until gate alignment."

"Fine," Candace said. "Sit down, shut up, and pay attention. The system does all the work anyways." Jackson and his crew had been watching Candace and her team align the gate every day for the last three weeks. If Jackson didn't know what he was doing already, this last time wouldn't help him. She didn't say that though. What was the point? His eyes tracked her movement and slid over her.

Jackson sat in the empty chair beside Candace. His eyes tracked her movement and slid over her. Candace watched and, when he was settled, she turned back to the console. A twitch of her eye accessed the outpost system via her clip. She glanced at the visitor tab and focused on it to bring up the manifest for this alignment. One hundred and three people, all human.

"Have you pulled up the visitor manifest?"

"Yup," he said.

Boredom was etched across every inch of his face. The next three years were going to suck for him.

"Okay, well, just follow along with what I'm doing."

In the three centuries since humanity had become a part of the intergalactic Empire, nearly all facets of technology across the galaxies had migrated to the clip and to the net. It was humanity's one great contribution. Only at the outposts had the technology not been fully integrated. Candace guessed it was just a matter of cost. Cheaper to keep the old control panels than upgrade the systems of every outpost across the whole of space.

She flipped three switches on the panel. One stopped the

Outpost from siphoning off power from the gate allowing it to leave standby mode, the other returned the Gate to normal function, and the last recalibrated the atmosphere in the hangar so humans could breathe.

As the vents opened, the sound of metal scraping on stone filled the hangar and Control Room. The still black void inside the gate's arch shimmered for a moment, like moonlight on the surface of a lake at midnight. Or at least, Candace thought it had. A slight vibration radiated across the control room. It reverberated from the metal instrument panel to the tips of her fingers. She waited for it to stop but it didn't. Nothing like this, not in all of the hundreds of transmissions she'd overseen, had happened before. At least not that she could recall.

It's nothing. Just my nerves. Candace put it from her mind and returned her focus to watching the gate align. The life support readout on her clip confirmed that the hangar had reached the correct air pressure and atmospheric make-up.

The clip indicated one life sign in the hangar. Jared should be in there finishing the sanitization process. She caught another flash from the gate out of the corner of her eye.

The control panel vibrated louder. She considered reporting these events and calling off the visitor transmission, but that would mean an inspection. An inspection would mean days or weeks stuck here waiting for the inspectors' report. Julia would kill her if that happened, and for what, a little tremor? It was probably nothing. Cable loose somewhere. Jackson can deal with that after she's gone. The clock in her head-up display flashed red.

TRAVIS

ravis Scanlon walked morosely beside his boyfriend Devon. They were headed to the recreation room, his least favorite place in the Outpost. On a normal day, Travis was happy to sit in his lab, comb through the data he had collected on the Avealus Gate, plan his next set of experiments, and correspond with his colleagues at the University on Xexal. Devon was an unexpected addition.

Travis had actually requested to be at Outpost 9106 — the only person ever to do so — *because* it was remote. He didn't want to be around other people unless he had to be. Then he met Devon and fell in love. Now he was being dragged to the Rec Room to socialize. It was certain to be filled with people. Thirty-two people from his crew and their thirty-two replacements. Even if they weren't all in there, it was still going to be too many. Fudge Candace for giving everyone the night off and unlocking the booze cart.

"Buck up," Devon said, showing off his perfect smile.

Why did he have to be so damned beautiful? Dirty blond hair cropped short, lean and muscular chest and arms. Travis nearly sighed at the sight of him, but smiled back instead. There was no need to be too cliché.

"You're lucky I love you," Travis responded in a low voice. They walked in silence for a moment, winding their way through the outpost. The dim yellow fluorescent bulbs provided the only light in the cavernous halls. Travis suspected the maintenance tunnels were even more cave-like, he'd always wanted to explore them but had never taken the time to do it. He wasn't even sure he had access to them. It didn't matter. In a few minutes his tour would be done, and in two days the gate would align to send him home.

Before he knew it, they had arrived at the rec room. Travis's pulse began to quicken, the familiar anxiety knowing its cue. A cacophony of known and unknown voices flowed out of the open door and into the hall. Travis stopped short. Devon took a few extra steps before stopping and seeing that Travis was no longer next to him.

Devon turned and said apologetically, "Let's forget it. We can just go chill in your room."

Travis managed a weak impression of a smile. *Good ol' Devon. Always taking care of me.* "No. We always do what I want to do. Come on, let's have a drink and play some pool." He gestured Devon forward with his hand. "Let's go." *Stupid Travis. He gave you an out. There was no need to be a martyr.*

The rec room was more crowded than Travis had thought possible. *When did this room get so small?* More than fifty people overflowed the tiny space. No stools or bar tables had any vacancies, and all of the virtual bowling lanes in the back were occupied. The heat was unbearable, and the only scent more potent than the mélange of alcohol was the pungent smell of human sweat.

Devon meandered slowly through the crowd as Travis followed. *Look straight ahead. Avoid the eyes. Don't count their feet. Don't think about exit strategies. This is for Devon. Remember that this is for Devon.*

Travis wished his boyfriend would pick up the pace. He needed to put his back against a wall. At least then he'd feel safe from one of six sides. Thankfully, the pool table near the left wall emptied as they approached it. Travis sped past Devon and took his place against the gray stone.

He glanced at Devon. His eyes were wide and his mouth was slightly agape. Maybe Devon really hadn't understood how much Travis detested crowds and people. Devon turned away.

A second later, a game invitation popped up on Travis's head-up display. When Travis glanced at "Accept," the invitation disappeared and a pool cue materialized in front of him. He grabbed it. This newer clip was truly something else. Even though the pool cue was just a digital projection sent from the metal disc on the back of his neck, the display accessed the rest of his central nervous system, meaning he could feel the weight and balance of the long piece of wood.

"You want to break, hon?" Devon asked.

Travis nodded. He glanced at the clock in the corner of his vision. The numbers were red. Fifteen minutes until the last gate transmission of his tour.

JACKSON

o what are you going to do with your freedom?" Jackson asked to fill the uncomfortable silence. *Three more years of this. Why did I agree to such a long tour?*

He watched Candace as he waited for his answer. Old, or at least oldish, but not ugly. Her hair looked greasy, like she could use a shower, but there was a hint of something beneath the uniform. He wondered if there would be anyone worth fucking while he was here. No one he'd seen during decontamination was of particular interest, but time and boredom would change that.

"Freedom?" Candace seemed puzzled by the word. *Could she be that stupid?*

"What are you going to do with your two days waiting for your gate off world? And after that?" he corrected, his tone purposely obnoxious.

"Ah," she answered. "Packing and then enjoying retirement."

Retire? How?

Some of his shock must have shown on his face, because hers changed from a blank expression of boredom to one of mild humor. She almost smiled.

"You seem a little young to retire," Jackson said.

"I am," she offered. Her eyes traced something invisible in front of her. She must be looking at something on her clip.

"Do you feel that?" Candace asked.

Jackson peered around, confused. Then he noticed it. A slight vibration in the floor. How had he not noticed that?

"Shit," he said and bent forward to push the deadlock switch and cut off the gate power.

"Don't," Candace said and held a hand up to block him. "It's fine. Power levels are still in the green. No other abnormalities."

"We have to report this," he said, surprised by the urgency and authority in his voice.

"We don't. It's happened before. It's fine. I've been doing this for twenty-four years. Plus, this lines up with the memo Tsoral sent. Trust me." She lowered her hand and took a deep breath.

Trust you? I don't fucking know you. But Jackson leaned back in his chair.

"Twenty-four years? Out here?" The thought of that made him nauseous. She must be ridiculous to do that.

"No, not out here. I did eighteen years on hub worlds. They had to bribe me with triple pay to take this post. No one else would do it." Candace laughed. "And I made them throw in my full pension to boot."

Well that explains the early retirement. Fuck. I should have tried that. I knew they were desperate for someone to take this post.

The room continued to vibrate. *This can't be good. No other outpost I'd worked at had vibrated during a gate alignment. Though, I've never been in the control room during alignments.*

"Are you sure the vibration is okay?" he asked. "We're supposed to deadlock the system and report this. We don't want to blow up the outpost."

"Look. You seem nice, and I'm sure you'll do a great job running this shithole when I'm gone, but I have been through some ten-thousand of these things with no issue. Trust me. I know what I'm doing. I mean, fuck, the gates have been around a thousand years and no outpost has ever blown up. Relax."

This didn't make Jackson feel any better. His pulse still raced, and the vibrations had his feet feeling numb. She was right though; she was in charge and she had the experience.

He shrugged. That seemed to pacify Candace, but he made sure to stay within reaching distance of the deadlock switch. If it was needed, he'd use it. Fuck her and her authority.

AEON

eon stood next to his friend Maggie and stared at the blond guy and his "boyfriend" as they bent over the pool table in the rec hall shooting at invisible balls. A wave of disgust coursed up his throat. It soured the flavor of the passable liquor that Outpost 9106 provided.

Look at those two. Every time the one with dark hair leaned over for his shot, the blond one would peek at his ass. Seriously? As if they weren't surrounded by other people. *Decent* people. At least the little dark-haired faggot was smart enough to be ashamed of himself.

Aeon finally peeled his eyes away from the couple, knowing that if he didn't, he would either vomit or walk over and knock their teeth out. When he turned back around, Maggie was gone. Aeon cursed the two queers under his breath. They fucked up his night with the only passable-looking woman in this dump.

He sipped more of the clear liquid and let the burn fill his chest. It had a calming effect. A clearing effect. A cleaning effect. Aeon imagined spitting the liquid into the nasty fags' eyes as retribution for cockblocking him. *Okay.* His eyes sweep the room searching for Maggie's signature red hair. *Let's find this bitch. I need to cleanse my palate.*

Aeon set his glass on the table and stood up from the stool, already planning his moves. He'd chat up the girl and then take her down into the maintenance tunnels. He was fairly sure only him and the other maintenance staff could access that area, and down there no one would interrupt him and Maggie like Caig did last night when Aeon had taken Maggie to his room.

"You feel that?" someone near him asked.

"The little shaking? Yeah. It's probably just the music." Another responded.

A moment later Aeon felt the vibration in the table his palm was resting on. A faint shiver skimmed along the surface of the liquid in the glass next to him. Faint, but there. He'd done four tours, all on backwater planets like this, and had never experienced anything like an earthquake.

He searched the room again, but now for signs that anyone else was as alarmed as he was. The noise in the room seemed louder than ever. Thirty different conversations all going on at once. Not one person appeared panicked. All he saw was a swirling mob of happy faces unmarred by worry. Maybe he was overreacting.

Aeon tried to slow his breathing and settle his heartbeat. His eye raked across the crowd again, more slowly this time, certain he wouldn't find anything. Then he paused on someone. *Wait. What is that?* Blondie was staring at him. In the other man's eyes Aeon saw the same concern and confusion. *Fuck.*

TRAVIS

What is going on? Why is the outpost shaking? It was an occurrence that would be fitting on almost any other world, especially ones with cities, or mass transit, or millions of people, but here on this rock it was not. Here, even the most minute tremor was something of note. Travis lifted his gaze and actually took in the room, more than the quick glances he'd allowed himself intermittently, trying to find reassurance that his judgment was completely compromised by his anxieties and fears. The faces all appeared the same though: a mix of joyful stupidity or contented inebriation, with no hint of the danger they were all in. Except for one. The burly man Travis had seen staring at them was watching him again, but he no longer seemed angry.

"Travis?" Devon asked. "You with me?"

Travis blinked and turned away from the burly man. *Why has he been staring at us all night? No. There are more important things to focus on.*

"Travis!"

He blinked again and found Devon waving his hand in front of his face. "Huh?"

"What's up with you?"

Travis's brow pulled up in confusion. "You don't feel that?"

Devon smiled nervously. "Feel what?"

Feel what? Feel what?! Travis put his hand on the green felt of the pool table and motioned for Devon to do the same. When Devon copied Travis, his smile faded.

"Do you feel it now?"

Devon nodded. "Why is the outpost shaking? Has it ever done this before?"

"No." The vibrations intensified under Travis's hand, becoming a low, audible drone. "It's never done this before."

Travis's mind started to whirl as it began to contemplate the cause or reason for this deviation from the norm. Had there been any aberrations in the gate readings? Was there something different about this transmission? The answer kept coming up no. If there had been, as second in command, he'd have been notified by the system automatically. So what was going on?

"Is it a big deal?"

"I don't know."

Travis wanted to believe it wasn't a big deal, that he was overreacting. Command had said the update might cause issues. So why was his chest tightening and his heart pounding so hard? It wasn't just the crowd and the noise, but those weren't helping him think clearly. He gripped the edge of the pool table to try and ground himself. He let the feel of the wood, metal, and felt consume his focus. *I'm here for Devon. I'm here for Devon. Plus, I have to get used to people because we will be back on Terra in a week.*

"It's probably nothing," Devon said as he lined up his next shot. It was technically Travis's turn, but Travis didn't care. He just wanted to get to Candace and the control room to find out what had happened.

"Yeah," Travis said placatingly.

CANDACE

"One minute until gate alignment," the robotic announcer's voice intoned.

Almost done. Candace focused on her heart beat. She let the steady rhythm of it calm her. It was an old trick. It grounded her in the moment — in the *right now*.

The light on the control panel turned yellow indicating the hundred and three people at the Avealus Gate on Vexal-7 were ready to enter. Candace glanced along the instrument panel. The priming light was off. Good. That meant the gate was ready.

"Showtime," Jackson said.

He said it every time. An image of taking a hammer to his smug face flashed across her mind. "Yes, it is," Candace said icily.

One minute and then I can go join the party. One minute and I'll be away from this idiot. She could see him still hovering over the deadlock switch. He seriously thought he knew better.

Maybe he was right. She knew he was right. It was a dumb risk to ignore the vibrations and the strange way the gate itself was behaving, but if she was wrong, if nothing was actually wrong, she could be sacrificing weeks or months away from Julia while Command conducted their investigation. They could even revoke her pension and bonus.

She'd seen it before. The company didn't like it when business was disrupted and money was lost. Old bosses had lost everything by making the cautious choice and it always turned out to be nothing. If that's what this was, all she'd worked for these last twenty-five years would be lost: her retirement, her future. Despite these consequences, the itch to press the button ratcheted up her arm.

"Thirty seconds until gate alignment."

Candace flipped the switch that signaled to the command team at the other gate that they were ready on their end. It was done. She had put flipping the last switch off as long as she could. Now it was too late to change her mind. The guests would be coming.

The vibrations suddenly increased. The floor shook. Dust trickled down into her hair. The sound of the weird buzzing grew louder and she could no longer pretend not to hear or feel it.

"Ten seconds until Avealus Gate alignment," said the announcer.

Inside the hangar, the gate flashed white again. The light on the panel turned green.

"Nine seconds."

The floor rocked beneath their feet. The control room hummed with electricity, almost as if it had a static charge. The air in the hangar had grown hazy and shimmered like a mirage rising up off the hot desert sand. Candace gazed into the darkness, focused on the gate. The black inside the giant archway seemed to glow. *That's not good.*

Something is wrong. Press the deadlock. Just press it. Julia will understand.

"Eight seconds."

Press it.

"Seven seconds."

Do it now!

Candace's skin tightened in anticipation. The beat of her

heart was wild. Sweat leaked from every pore. This wasn't right. None of this was supposed to happen. None of this had ever happened before. She *should* press the deadlock. Just to be safe. If she was right, she would save dozens of lives.

But if she was wrong? If she was wrong, risked her pension. Her retirement. *Julia.* Wouldn't more warning lights be going off if something was wrong? In the last thousand years, there've been millions of successful transmissions and nothing catastrophic has happened. Why would it happen now?

You know. You know it's a possibility because they have a deadswitch. They told you that the only reason to press the deadswitch was in the event of a complete system failure. A breach. It might never have happened, but there's a reason it exists. So follow protocol. Do your job. Even if they take your money. Even if they blame it all on you.

"Six seconds."

Candace shifted her stance. It was like insects were crawling over her body. She glanced at Jackson. His face was pale and clammy. He looked ready to vomit.

"Five seconds."

"Four seconds."

If I'm going to do it, now is the moment.

"Three seconds.

I should push the deadswitch. I should stop this. Something isn't right. What if — The Avealus Gate flashed white. Orbs of blue and green pop across her vision leaving transparent glowing images along her retinas. The light was so vivid she could taste it.

"Two seconds."

"Gate transmission commencing."

The indicator turned green. People would be coming through now. Candace hated this part when she was the one traveling through a gate. You stood in front of a black wall that was like a micro-thin curtain. Once you walked through, you were instantly on another planet. There was no physical sensation. No time passed. At least, that was how it seemed. It wasn't the truth though. Once you passed through the surface of that curtain, you disappeared for 1.2 seconds. No one knows why this happens. Where you went. How you got there. You just vanished for 1.2 seconds and then reappeared with no sense of the lost time. Candace hated that.

There was too much unknown about the Zurathel Transit Corp's Gates. Because of their history of being so safe and reliable, no one questioned how or why they worked. For centuries, before humanity joined the Empire, people had tried to understand how they worked, to improve them, to replicate them, but when no one could accomplish this they gave up. It didn't matter how they worked, just that they did. The gates became a part of society, so commonly used now that only weirdos like Travis bothered to study them.

"Prepare to indicate receipt," she said to Jackson.

Jackson's hand drifted away from the deadlock switch and dropped to his lap. His eyes went vacant, and Candace knew his mind was hovering over the button on his clip.

One second stretched to two. The Avealus Gate's ominous glow permeated the control room. The milky haze hung in the air as it hissed and popped. The floor hummed louder with the vibrations. Candace wondered if the whole Outpost would be shaken apart. If it kept up, the outer walls could crack and everyone would be killed by the vacuum of the barren planet or by the extreme heat and radiation of the star it orbited. It was too late to do anything more than hope now.

Two seconds became three . . . then four . . . then five. Still no guests walked through the gate. She glanced at Jackson and saw the same worry written on his face. Her heart thrashed around her ribcage like an animal trying to claw its way out. *I should have deadlocked the system. Something is wrong.* She thought of all the guests who should have been here already. *Dear God, I've killed them all.*

Five seconds. Six. Seven. Eight.

"Should we do something?" Jackson asked, sounding panicked.

"Do what?"

"I don't know. Something. There has to be something we can do. Can we contact the other gate? Maybe they haven't gone through yet."

"One minute until Avealus Gate desynchronization." The cheerfulness of the female voice seemed to be mocking them.

Candace groaned. "Just shut up. Let's give it another second before we panic. I'm not getting stuck on this shithole of a planet one day longer than I need to be."

Thirteen seconds had passed. *I'm gonna have to deadlock it now. I have to protect the outpost and the gate. Fuck. I should have let Jackson deadlock it from the start. Now the guests are probably all dead. I'm going to go to jail for this. I'll never get to see Julia again.*

The Avealus Gate flashed again. Candace's clip pinged. Outpost 9106 had registered a new lifeform. She rose slightly from her chair and looked out into the hangar and through the shimmery haze she saw someone passing through the gate.

"Thank God," Candace said. All the muscles in her body unclenched. She moved her hand away from the deadlock switch. When had she reached for it?

Jackson sighed. It sounded distant to her ears. Her clip continued to ping as more and more visitors passed through the gate.

"There is a six-hour layover between gate transmissions," the female voice intoned. "Please feel free to rest in the designated wait area. To prevent the spread of off-world pathogens, we ask that you do not leave the isolation zones. Thank you for understanding."

"Well, that was fun, but let's not do it again," Jackson said.

They both laughed.

"Fucking a," she said. "I'm so glad this is over."

The counter on her clip read one hundred and four new life forms.

"That's all of them," Jackson said, yet the expression of concern never left his face. His hand swayed toward the deadlock switch.

The vibrations hadn't ceased. They had intensified. The air shook with them.

She peered through the glass out into the hangar. "Do i—"

The air crackled. Candace gasped as the hangar exploded. Bricks shattered in a cloud of dust. Limbs and blood catapulted in all directions. The floor cracked, ruptured, and pitted. The stone structure of the Avealus Gate fractured.

The ancient relic now resembled nothing more than shattered bone.

A shockwave struck the control room. The walls bowed and the glass rippled. The force threw Candace backwards. She slammed into the floor and rolled. A searing pain pierced her head and darkness enveloped her.

DEVON

All Devon could see was blood. It coated the ground, the wall, the door. Sally lay behind the bar wailing. A woman pressed a shirt to the stump where Sally's arm had been as another wrapped a belt above the wound to make a makeshift tourniquet. Devon had seen it happen. The explosion had knocked everyone to the ground and in a flash, the rec room door had slammed shut. It happened so quickly that Sally hadn't even realized she'd lost her arm until seconds later, but Devon had realized it and all he'd been able to do was stand and watch.

Chaos swarmed around him now. A scream trapped in his throat.

This is no big deal. A door malfunction. That's it. Nothing to worry about. Devon knew that was a lie even as he thought it.

What about that shaking? What about when the whole floor had rocked underneath our feet, nearly knocking them over? It felt like half the outpost blew up.

"What the fuck is going on?" someone shouted.

Devon couldn't get his thoughts together enough to form a response. There was too much noise. Too many people. The invisible weight of the crowd was crushing him. Had the room become smaller?

Travis. The thought was a lifeline. A direction. A purpose.

His boyfriend pounded his fists against the metal door. Their only exit out of the recreation room. It was futile. The door wouldn't open. Not until a rescue came, and that could take hours.

Someone tugged at his sleeve, but Devon's attention was locked on Travis. They tugged harder and then the hand gripped his arm and forced him to turn. Devon blinked at the person, finally comprehending what was happening. A gruff man from the new crew stood barely an inch away from Devon. The reek of alcohol wafted up Devon's nostrils. Bile and vomit surged up his throat. He swallowed it back down.

"Does he" — the man motioned to Travis with his head — "know what's going on?"

Devon tried to speak, but his throat was too dry. The man handed him a glass of clear liquid. Devon blinked at it for a long moment before taking it. He downed it in one long gulp. The liquor burned him from mouth to stomach and parted the fog that had gathered around his brain.

"N-no." Devon paused and tried to think. "Maybe. I don't know." He watched Travis beat his fists vainly against the immovable metal.

"Well, go check for fuck's sake."

Devon walked over to Travis. His legs were stiff and disconnected from the rest of his body, and even though Travis was only a few feet away, it might as well have been a mile. Devon nearly slipped on the blood soaked floor and only kept from falling because the other man following closely behind grabbed him and held him up. When he had regained his feet, the other man shoved him harshly, causing him to stumble into Travis, who jumped. What he saw in Travis's eyes was more than Devon could comprehend. It was the death wail coming from Sally made flesh.

"Travis," Devon whispered. His hand gripped Travis's wrist, ignoring the blood coating it. "Let's get you out of the crowd."

Travis looked back at him with distant, terrified eyes and didn't resist as Devon steered him through the crowd.

"Water," Devon said to the new guy. "I'm sorry. I don't know your name."

"Aeon," the man said, eyes darting everywhere but at Devon or Travis.

"Thank you, Aeon. Water? Please?"

Aeon didn't move. Devon knew the man's name and reputation and wasn't happy to finally be able to put a face to both. The disgust on Aeon's face confirmed everything he'd heard, but now wasn't the time for arguments. Travis needed help.

"Please."

Aeon ground his teeth and walked away. Devon hoped for water. He and Travis moved through the crowd which parted as they walked, hurling question after question at them, so many and all at once that Devon couldn't make sense of any. The words were as much a blur as the panicked faces crowding in around them.

Finally, they made it to the other side, breaking through and moving quickly to an empty corner in the far end of the room. It no longer seemed like fifty-odd people in the room, but five hundred. The heat from all the bodies was stifling. The air was heavy. *God dammit will someone shut Sally up!*

When they reached the corner, Devon sat Travis on the ground so that his back was pressed against the far wall and then began to examine him more closely. His face was pale and his pupils were as large as dinner plates. Blood coated his hands and shirt. Whether it was Travis's or Sally's, Devon wasn't sure. It was shock Devon was worried about anyway. He didn't like the look in Travis's eyes, his utter lack of response. If Travis was going into shock, there was less than nothing that he could do for him but he would try.

Now that they were separated from the crowd, Devon began to make out the dissonant chants the cacophony of voices bellowed.

"Let us out."

"Open the door."

"Oh God, we're trapped."

"Are we under attack?"

His gaze swept over them. Everyone either was tending to Sally or making panicked circles around the crowd in front of the door. The distance did nothing to blunt the volume of the voices.

"Hey?" a female voice asked from somewhere nearby.

Devon turned toward the voice. Rita stood a few away. Her skin the color of sour milk, glistening with a thin sheen of sweat. She was one of the only people on the crew that Travis tolerated. Other than himself.

"What's up, Rita?" Devon didn't like how much panic there was in his own voice.

"You're the network rep, right?"

You know I am. "Yeah. Why? You don't think this is a network malfunction, do you? Listen I have to help Trav —"

"Is your clip working?" she interrupted.

At that moment, Aeon returned carrying half a dozen water bottles in his arms. His face a mask of fear.

"What?" Devon asked. "I told you I need to help Travis. He's in shock."

"Just check it," Rita snapped.

Devon blinked. There was nothing. The date and time were gone from his field of vision. He tried to call up the directory to call Candace, but nothing happened. None of the clip features or fields populated. His HUD was missing. The network was gone, and since the clip functioned on the network, the clip didn't work. He was completely disconnected from the rest of the outpost. A feeling of utter emptiness filled him.

Can I be afraid now?

CANDACE

andace groaned. The taste of copper filled her mouth, and her nose was packed full and pointed in a new direction. Dried blood caked her lips shut and she had to peel them apart so she could breathe.

The world around her seemed to be holding its breath. Sparks arced lazily off the console, the fluorescent lights above flickered and swayed. She grunted and made it onto her hands and knees. Her head throbbed. Pain lanced at her temples, her eyes, her cheeks, her nose like needles made of lightning. Candace's vision went gray at the edges and vomit erupted from her mouth. She coughed the last of it out and stared absently at the foamy sick between her hands.

"You alive?" someone croaked.

Gingerly, Candace turned her head to find the originator of the voice. Jackson lay against the wall across the room. Blood soaked half his face, the skin that showed was pale and sallow. He was more of a corpse than a man. Only the heat in his gaze marked him as alive.

"Clearly," she answered. "You?"

"Sadly."

He rubbed the blood away from his eye, but fresh blood

trickled down from his hairline to replace it. *Shit. I need to do something about his bleeding. What though?* Thinking made her head throb and her stomach roil. Vomit erupted again, but it was less this time. When her stomach ceased spasming, she tried to stand. Her body did not want to listen. It took her a while to find her feet.

Bang! Bang! Bang!

Candace gently shook her head to try to clear it. *Fuck. Who turned the volume in my head up so high?*

Bang!

The noise wasn't in her mind. She searched for the sound and saw that the blast shield quivered with each bang sending bits of debris down from the edges of the metal-covered windows. Was something hammering on it from inside the hangar? *That's impossible. No one could have lived through that blast.*

"That's a foot of solid steel," she whispered. She looked to Jackson for confirmation of what she saw but the sight of him drove the noise from her mind. When he wiped his head again, she saw with clear eyes how deep and long the laceration on his scalp was. She wasn't sure, but she thought she could see the white of bone beneath the flap of loose skin. *Shit.* She limped across the room to the first aid box hanging on the wall and tried to pull it down, but when it didn't budge, she settled for pulling out all of the bandages, gauze, iodine, and tape inside before making her way over to where Jackson sat.

"Shit, you look like death," she mumbled to him.

"How bad is it?"

Candace took the gauze and dabbed at the blood on his face. Three cuts lashed their way from his eyebrows to his hairline. Wiping the blood did in fact reveal the white of bone. She was glad when the wound began to well and drip again. She added another gauze to the cuts and applied pressure.

"It isn't so bad," she lied. "I don't know the last time this stuff was changed out, but it should work. You'll be fine," she said, trying to assure herself more than him.

He needs stitches and antibiotics. I don't want to think about the kind of germs lingering here.

"This will hurt," she said and poured iodine on wounds. Jackson hissed and cursed as she pressed a thick stack of gauze onto the cuts.

"Hold these in place."

Jackson lifted his hand and held the stack while Candace wrapped long bandages around his head. When she was done, she stood up and stepped away. Her chest unlocked and her breath vacated in a rush. The room smelled of blood and vomit and dust. It was silent except for the sound of their breathing.

Bang!

Candace screamed and her hand flew up to cover her mouth.

"Fuck."

The metal of the blast shield held. Candace inched toward the control board, waiting for another impact. Upon reaching the long console, she paused. It only took a glance to know what had happened. Quarantine protocol had gone into effect. Every room had been sealed off. The air in the hangar and the hallways had been vented and sealed to create a vacuum. Nothing could — or would — survive in those hallways for long.

I need to survey the damage. Figure out what happened and what our options are. Candace wished she could lift the blast shield to see the state of the hangar and the gate. No one in the hangar could be alive. If the explosion hadn't killed them, the lack of atmosphere would have.

Fuck. The memory of Jackson reaching for the deadlock switch flashed across her mind. *Why did I stop him? How could I have let this happen? All those people. I killed —*

"What the hell happened?" Jackson limped closer to Candace, a zombie hobbling as best he could. All of the humor had bled out of him, rendered onto the stained white cotton piled on the ground. She looked at him and shrugged.

"Some sort of explosion," Candace whispered.

"No shit," Jackson shouted. "But what fucking caused it? Were we attacked? Was it the Cysarian's?"

No, she thought. *Maybe. I don't know. The gates have never failed before.* "How the fuck should I know? The Cysarian's haven't ever done anything this massive before, and if it was them, why here? We aren't an important route."

Candace blinked and tried to pull up the video feed of the hangar on her clip. She thought of the command, but nothing happened. When it didn't work, she attempted to pull up the application manually. Nothing. The entire heads-up display was gone; the Net was gone. The memory of the explosion raced through her mind: The stone arch shattering. The floor cracking apart. The shockwave obliterating all of those people.

All that blood.

They were completely cut off.

"My clip isn't working?" Her voice sounded faint. Images of red filled her mind: People liquidated in an instant. A wall of red suspended in the air speeding toward them.

"What?" A pause. "Shit." Another pause. "What does that mean?"

"I don't know," she said. "I think it means the network is down." *Which also means the gate is toast.* The pathways of the Zurathel Transit Gates provided network access across galaxies to places the network relays couldn't reach, even when the gates weren't aligned. There was no place in the six galaxies of the Empire that didn't receive network signaling. The gates guaranteed that.

Candace gasped as she processed the implications. *If people don't know how old the gates were, how they were made, or even what they were made of, could they even be fixed? Probably not.* That meant — shit — they had no way of communicating out to other stations. Did they just become another dead lane, left here to starve and die. In all her years with the transit company, she'd received no training for a gate shutdown. If there was an explosion, a bioweapon attack, or a traveler carrying an unknown pathogen, and quarantine protocol kicked in, the gates were expected to be there. So was the network. There was no contingency for a situation like this and no way to communicate with headquarters to ask what to do.

Bang!

Candace jolted.

"What is that?" Jackson asked.

"Secondary explosions? Don't worry. This room is meant to withstand a thermonuclear blast. A small one, at least. We should be safe here till rescue comes. Quarantine must have kicked in." She walked away from the console and began pacing to calm herself.

"We need to check the gate," Jackson said, turning towards her.

Gods was he stupid.

Bang!

Candace shook her head. "We can't. You know that. That shield is the only thing protecting us. We can't open it."

"That isn't true. The glass is six inches thick and blast proof. We don't have to open it for long. Just long enough to assess the damage."

"Stop," Candace shouted. "You have no clue if the glass is still intact. If it's shattered, we're dead. That is the whole point of the quarantine protocol. It keeps us safe from the shit we don't know about."

The atmosphere in the room shifted. Jackson's eyes flashed, and he growled. His face contorted and his glance darted all around the room. Slowly he began to shake his head. Candace watched and waited, anticipating violence.

Finally Jackson spoke. "If the gate is really destroyed, then no one can get here to help us. Is it your plan to just sit here while we starve to death?"

Candace stared at him for a long time, really tried to see him. Just a man, scared, weak, and stupid.

"Just shut up," Candace said. "Until this is over, I'm still in charge."

She walked a few steps away when Jackson said, "Fuck that." He lunged at the control panel and slammed his hand against the switch that lifted the shield. Candace didn't have time to flinch. The metal plates lifted and the hum flooded in.

Candace shrieked as pain ripped through her brain, like her skull was being shredded apart from the inside. She clapped her hands over her ears. It did no good. The hum soaked through her skin, flooded her mouth and nose, suffocating her.

"Close it," she shouted. "Now!"

Rage consumed her, seeping into every corner of her mind, filling her with the urge to kill him. Break him. She was in fucking charge. *Not Jackson! Her!* And he had no right to disobey her.

In three strides Candace was beside Jackson, her hand cocked back to strike him. His hands were over his ears. Blood leaked from his tear ducts. Candace didn't care. She paused mid-strike when she caught movement out of the corner of her eye and glanced through the dirty glass out into the hangar.

The Gate was cracked. Long fissures spiderwebbed across it like varicose veins. Candace worried a gentle breeze would cause it to collapse at any moment, but it wasn't as bad as she'd expected. The floor was worse. Beneath the ocean of crimson and limbs, the cracked gray floor had risen up in places and split open in others.

A chunk of the wall was missing. Where the door to the waiting area had been was a gaping, jagged hole. A trail of blood led into the dark passage. As her hand moved to shut the shield, she saw something move. Or thought she did. But there was nothing there. No living person moved within the devastated hangar, yet she was certain something was in there. She could feel it, and somehow she knew it could feel her too.

Candace flipped the switch and the blast shield slammed

shut. The hum vanished and Candace let out a breath of air. Her heart ran at the speed of hummingbird wings.

The noise was gone, but the rage remained, and she liked it. It was obvious now where the anger was coming from. She could feel it flowing into her from whatever was beyond the metal wall, flooding her veins like a new supply of oxygen. "If you try anything like that again, I will kill you."

TRAVIS

Travis came around slowly, bit by bit, but he wished he hadn't. At least the screeching had stopped. Travis did not want to think about what that meant, and he did not want to think about the blood coating his hands and arms. His hands ran absently over the roughness of his pants. The crowd milled around aimlessly like waddling ducks quacking at each other, but a few, too many for sure, stood near him waiting for answers he didn't have.

Devon, Rita, and others watched him closely. The mass around him grew as he woke. Their eyes bored into him as if he was sitting naked and was a spectacle worth gawking at.

I wish everyone would just go away.

"Travis? Do you know what's going on?" Devon asked gently.

"This is going nowhere. Let's just get the door open." The gruff man, Aeon tried to pull Devon towards the door, but Devon shook the hand off.

"Shut up. Just shut up. I am tired of hearing from you," Devon said. Then he pointed a finger at Travis. "If anyone knows what is going on here it's him. It's his whole job. So just be quiet and let him explain."

Aeon's face grew redder with each word, his hands turned white as he clenched his fists tighter.

"But I don't," Travis heard himself say. Delicately, he stood up. His legs shook and his muscles spasmed. The room had gone from too noisy to too quiet. Everyone was watching him, waiting for him to have some sort of answer, but he didn't have one. All those eyes were like hands squeezing his skull.

Travis began to pace. Moving helped. It calmed and centered him. *Think Travis. Think. Remember. What happened?* His mind carefully recounted the moments before he blacked out. He remembered the door coming down, saw it slice through Sally. The blood — *nope. Go back further.* He remembered the explosion. The way the floor shook. The brief sound of . . . a*n attack? Did the explosion cause a malfunction in the door system? If that was it, then why weren't their clips connecting to the network?*

Devon walked around in front of him, forcing him to stop walking. "Travis?"

"What?"

"Are you okay?"

Travis laughed mockingly. "Don't be thick. Are *you* okay?"

Devon's eyes dropped to the floor and he pouted.

"Sorry," Travis said. "Look. I don't know what is going on, but I have some ideas. First thing I need to know is why our clips stopped working and why we can't connect to the network. You're the network rep, do you know why?"

Devon scanned the room before turning to Aeon. "Is Aerica in here? She's your crew's net rep right?"

"No," Aeon said. "I haven't seen her all day."

"Damn," Devon said. He ran a hand over his face. "Well, the net is transmitted through the gate. The relay here at the outpost broadcasts the signal to our clips and gives us our secure connection, but even if the relay goes down, the clips should still be able to link directly to the transmission since we are so close to the gate. Since it's happening to all of us, it can't be a hardware issue with the clips themselves. That just leaves the

Avealus Gate. Even if we were deadlocked, we should still get a signal."

"Stop dancing around it and just say it," Aeon growled.

Devon let out a huff and bit his lip before meeting Travis's eye. "The only thing I can think of is that the gate is gone."

That's what I thought. Fuck.

"Okay," Travis said. "Okay, okay, okay . . ."

"But," Rita said, "how is that possible?"

"I don't know," Travis said. "It shouldn't be."

Thousands of beings from hundreds of species have been trying to figure out the origin and mechanics of the ancient gates for millennia. None of them had gotten anywhere. Dating them was impossible because no matter what you did, you couldn't damage them enough to pull a sample. Explosives, acids, lasers. Not even a scrape of dust flaked off.

Travis had thought his teachers were exaggerating when they'd told him as much during his university studies. He'd come to this place, hoping his research would allow him to surpass his predecessors. Much like them, his hope overshadowed the outcome. So what caused it to happen now?

"Well, that's just great. Just fucking great." Aeon flipped a nearby table, sending it crashing to the floor and scattering the glasses that had been on top of it before turning and stalking away into the crowd.

"Gosh, I wish I could flipping talk to Candace," Travis said to himself.

Devon's eyes went out of focus. Travis recognized the vacant look as the one worn by someone interacting with their clip.

"Did something change with your clip?" Travis asked and tried his own but the display was absent. Nothing.

A weak, meandering smile twitched at the corners of Devon's mouth.

"I think —" Devon stopped, licked his lips then stared Travis right in his eyes. "I think I might know how to talk to Candace. It's one in a million, but it's the best I can think of."

A feeling of hope swelled in his chest but Travis tried to squash it. Hope would be deadly if it didn't work out.

"What is it?" Devon paused with his mouth hanging open slightly.

Devon grabbed Travis by the hand and led him through the crowd. "It will be easier if I just show you."

CANDACE

The clang of metal on metal reverberated through the control room. Shattered pieces of chair littered the floor.

"Shit! Shit!" Jackson shouted as he slammed the metal chair against the sealed door.

Candace watched from her spot on the floor. The urge to strangle Jackson filled her like water pouring into a cup. *Why won't he fucking stop?* All he was doing was making a mess, wearing himself out, and treading on her last nerve.

"It's magnetically sealed, dumb ass," she repeated. He didn't respond but continued throwing the chair against the unwavering barrier.

"Jackson."

Nothing.

"Jackson!"

That was it. She stood and moved behind him quietly. When he swung the mangled chair back over his shoulder — it was only two legs and the seat now — Candace reached out, pulled it from his grasp and threw it across the room.

"Enough! Just, enough."

Jackson turned around. He towered over her. His chest heaved and his eyes burned with hatred. She could see the spreading sweat stains on his shirt and feel the heat rising off of him. The scent wafting up her nostrils reminded her of sewage.

"Back up," Candace said. "Now."

"Make me," he growled.

Fine. Her knee crushed into his scrotum. He inhaled sharply. Gagging and wheezing noises gurgled from his throat as he gripped his groin. Jackson stumbled back, slipped on a broken off leg of the chair and fell. Candace backpedaled and picked up a leg herself in case Jackson intended to press his luck.

"Are we done?" she asked. Her rage was ebbing, and fear was leaking in to replace it.

The thing in the hangar banged against the blast shield. *I wish I could knee it in the nuts too.*

"Answer me, Jackson. Are we done?"

Jackson's face filled with utter hatred as he curled up in the fetal position, but he nodded. Then his eyes went wide and he vomited green foam onto the dusty gray stone.

Candace knew this wasn't done, but it was good enough for now. She was going to keep the little bat close at hand though.

She moved backward in an arc. When the wall touched her shirt, she let herself slide down. "We're in lockdown, dip shit," she said.

Bang!

"The doors are magnetically sealed. They won't open until a rescue team arrives. Freaking out isn't going to help us. So sit down, get comfortable, and be patient."

"Wait? You saw the Gate." Jackson rasped. "It's fucked. No one can come through."

Candace stared at him for a few seconds. He was so pathetic. "No, there isn't going to be a rescue team," she said coldly.

"So you're just going to let us die?"

"Yes. Sorry."

Jackson deflated back into a ball on the floor. They sat in silence, the quiet only punctuated by the occasional bang from the thing in the hangar or a painful groan from Jackson.

Static hissed on the speakers above her. It crackled and went dead.

"What was that?" Jackson croaked.

Candace was about to say she didn't know when a familiar voice spoke to her through the speaker.

"— dace. Hello. Can you hear me?" Travis's next words were garbled. "Shut up, everyone. Candace. If you can hear me, please let me know."

"How!" Candace shouted.

"There should be a handheld receiver on the control panel somewhere. It's a little metal box with a wire on the bottom that connects to the console," Travis answered. The speaker reverted back to static.

"Get up and look for it!" Candace ordered.

She was on her feet and at the console a second later. Jackson was slower. He hobbled to the opposite end of the console.

What the fuck does a handheld receiver look like? Candace had gotten so used to the console that she'd stopped appreciating how big it was. A twenty-foot long counter of monitors, dials, buttons, knobs, lights, and switches. Small holes were scattered across the surface and cabinets underneath. She gripped the metal chair leg as she scanned the console and searched the cabinets. *Why don't they train us for this stuff?*

"I think I got it," Jackson called from his end of the console.

When she reached Jackson, she yanked the receiver from his hand. It was an oddly-shaped metal box the size of an apple with a plastic mesh on the front and black button on one side. She pressed the button and was amazed to hear static come over the speaker.

"Hello?" she said into the mesh. Only static answered.

"T-take your thumb off the button," Jackson said. She lifted her thumb. It was harder to do than she expected. The static ended and silence prevailed.

"Cee," Travis said. "Dang it, it's good to hear from you."

She clicked the button. "How are you holding up?"

There was a moment of quiet. "We are good, but I got fifty scared people holed up in the rec room with me. What the heck is going on?"

Candace set down the box and ran a hand through her messy hair. She licked her lips. Her mind buzzed with so many conflicting choices. She couldn't tell him the truth. Would Travis believe a lie? The man knew so much more than her about how the outposts operated. Candace could see Jackson watching, his eyes moving between her and the box. The moment stretched. Her fingers squeezed the chair leg harder. She narrowed her eyes at him and picked up the box.

"There was a small explosion in the hangar. Dropped us into lockdown status. It's nothing to worry about." She was surprised by how calm she sounded. It almost made the words seem true.

"Small explosion? What the fuck are you playing at?" Jackson said.

"Shut up, Jackson," she said.

"Listen, you cunt. I'm done with this." Jackson reached for the receiver but Candace pulled it away. "Tell them what the fuck is going on. They have a right to know."

Candace slammed the metal chair leg she carried against the bottom of the console leaving a small dent in the console base. The boom echoed around the room. Its message, she hoped, was clear.

"I am not going to create a panic," she said. "There is nothing we can do. *Nothing.* Getting them worked up is just going to make things worse."

The speaker popped and hissed.

"Hey, Candace?" Travis's voice sounded different, clearer, and all of the background noise was gone.

"It's just me now. There is a way to manually plug your clip into the box. Then we can speak normally. All you have to do is lift up the camera drone in the front of the clip and pull out the little metal piece underneath. Once you do that, plug it into the small hole at the bottom of the box."

Candace did as she was told. It was weird to blindly dig at the metal disk implanted on the back of her neck. It was like fingers were rooting around in her spine, but once the camera had been pulled out, the device came out easily. She plugged the wireless receiver into the little slot like she was instructed. There were three soft pops. It sounded like they were in her ears, but they were actually in her mind.

"All done," she said.

"Okay. Please tell me the truth. What is going on? Really?" Travis's voice was terse but still polite.

"I told you what was really going on." It was hard to keep the anger out of her voice, but she pushed the emotion down.

"Then why is the network down?" Travis said.

"I don't know. Maybe the sync got damaged in the blast. Ask your boyfriend. That is his job after all."

There was another long pause. "I already did. Devon said that the net would only go down if the gate was destroyed."

Candace forced a laugh that carried over into her words. "The gate? Destroyed?" She stopped as the laughter took over. "Yeah. How would that happen? Could it?"

Travis said nothing. *Come on Travis. Let the seed germinate.*

"I just — " he started. " Look, you're not talking to the crowd. It's me. Tell me the truth and I'll believe you."

Without missing a beat Candace said, "I am telling you that." She took a deep breath and shoved her shaking hand into her pocket. "Listen. Lockdown is gonna suck. Ration food and water. Keep people calm, and we will get through this. We just need to be patient."

"Candace —"

"Enough! Enough, Travis. Listen! I am still in charge here. So do as you're told and hunker down."

The tension in the silence that followed grew with each passing moment. Candace waited for an explosion of anger from him or from Jackson as he paced back and forth next to her. She was surrounded on all sides by people who didn't understand.

They were in real danger. They were all going to die here, either because of the thing in the hangar or starvation, but they didn't need to die afraid.

When Travis didn't say anything more, she let the smile on her face drop. Slowly the muscles in her face, shoulders, and hands began to relax. The shaking of her fingers grew worse, though. *Fucking adrenaline.*

Jackson turned and walked across the room. He reached the far wall, he lay with his back to her, and curled in a fetal position.

Whatever monster was in the hangar continued its repeated assault on the blast shield.

"Shut up!" Candace said. "Fuck. I get it."

TRAVIS

F UDGE! Fudging flipping — ugh!

Devon sat next to Travis, his head resting on Travis's shoulder. All around him, the others sat quietly or mumbled to those near them. The stench of blood, feces, and piss grew every minute. It was like the mood of the rec room made manifest.

None of the recent events made sense. It wasn't supposed to be possible. *Just because you've never heard of the network going down doesn't mean it hasn't happened.* When Travis had told the assembled masses this news, they had taken it with stoic grace, shambled off to find places to comfortably wait, but even in the beginning, there had been those who had grumbled about the unfairness of their current situation. That number had risen as the hours ticked by.

It took everything he had to keep his own panic in check. The room seemed to shrink a little every time he glanced around to check the mood. The constant light and inability to know the time made it all worse, but nothing was as bad as his growing doubt. As the hours ticked by, Travis began to wonder why the rescue hadn't come or why the network hadn't come back on. It wasn't right. If Candace was telling the truth, this would have been resolved quickly.

Travis's muscles and joints strained as he shifted in his spot on the floor. Across the room Aeon sat with six others huddled around him. Something about the way they were grouped together made the acid in Travis's stomach crawl up his throat.

"Pssst," Travis whispered to Devon.

Devon blinked rapidly and glanced around as if searching for some new catastrophe. "What's up?" he asked loudly.

"Shh. How long do you think we've been in here?"

"Too long." Devon adjusted his position and then resettled his head on Travis's shoulder.

"Seriously. How long?"

"I don't know. Six or seven hours? Maybe longer?"

"I was thinking closer to twelve. The rescue team should have been here ages ago. I don't think anyone's coming."

"Have you talked to Candace? Has she given us an update?"

"No. I'm starting to think she lied from the start."

"Why would she lie?"

"I don't know," Travis said. "It doesn't make any sense. If we were under attack, she'd have given us a warning to keep us on our guard, and if the gate really is gone —"

Travis shut his eyes and took a long slow breath. "If the gate is gone, why would she keep us locked in here? She could manually lift the lockdown and let us out so we could die comfortably. Why leave us here? I wish I could just see the gate. Maybe there is something I can do to at least get the network back?" The words just spilled out of him. But instead of making him feel better, instead of organizing his thoughts or making him sound crazy, it had the opposite effect. He needed to be out of this room.

Travis spaced out, worst-case scenarios flying through his mind. When he came to, he realized that Devon was staring at his hands instead. He wore his normal concentration face, a look that was usually adorable. Now it made the color drain from his face.

"What is it?" Travis asked.

"I'm —" Devon started. "I think I have an idea for how to get us out of here."

"How? The quarantine protocols can't be overridden except from the control room, and I don't think Candace will allow that. Without the use of her clip I don't think she'd even know how."

"I can't do anything about that, but I think it is possible to manually sync your clip with the outpost controls. You should be able to manually override individual doors and reset simple systems. We might even be able to get the gate powered up again," Devon said. His eyes glowed with joy.

Travis gaped at him, then he noticed the sudden silence around them. Everyone in the rec room was staring at them. Everyone had heard Devon speaking. Half the room looked shocked, the other half hopeful. Travis didn't know which expression made him more nervous.

"No. The more I think about it, the more I'm convinced I can do it."

"Devon," Travis interjected. "Shut up, please."

Devon did. Travis knew his boyfriend wasn't an idiot, and if he understood the hunger and fear and anger he saw in the crowd then Devon had too.

Across the room Aeon stood. A red-headed woman yanked at his sleeve trying to pull him back down to the floor. His group scanned anxiously around. Travis thought that they were checking the emotional climate of the rest of the room.

"Do you think we are gonna let you fags kill us all?" Aeon shouted. The word fag was like a needle popping Travis's ear drum. In the echo of Aeon's vitriol, all he could hear was the thunder of blood and a steely hissing.

"Excuse me?" Rita asked rising to stand between Aeon and Travis. "Who the fuck do you think you are?"

"Sit down," Aeon said. "Be a good girl." His tone was pleasant, but the threat was evident.

Three others stood between Rita and Aeon. Travis followed them to his feet.

"Come on," Travis said. "None of this bickering is getting us anywhere. You all heard Devon. If he's right, then I should be able to get the gate working, maybe just enough to get the net back. And if we get the net back, then we can guarantee that help is coming. There is no danger."

"No danger says you," Aeon spoke coldly. "But you aren't in charge. You don't even know what's actually going on. Candace says that we need to stay here. Who are you to say differently?"

"Yeah," one of his companions chimed in. "What if you open the door and all our air gets sucked out? Or some weird disease gets in?"

Frustration bubbled up in Travis. *How could they all be so stupid?*

Thankfully, Rita spoke so he didn't have to. "What if? *What if?* We could play that stupid game all shitting day. Could nasty shit happen if we open the door? Sure. But this might be the only chance we have. The alignment with the planet Virgo was hours ago! They should have sent a rescue crew. Where are they?"

"I don't se —" Aeon began.

"If we stay locked up here we are going to die. Sure as the sun rises," Travis said. "I'm going through the door. If you want to stop me, do it. If the gate is working and the net being down is just malfunction of the relay or something, then no harm done. We'll get the problem fixed and get back on with our lives, but if it's as bad as I think it is, I want to get working on solving the issue before we all waste away to nothing."

Travis scowled at Aeon, not wanting to reveal his anxiety. Devon squeezed Travis's hand. Travis let the warmth of Devon's touch center him. Aeon took two steps across the room and stopped. Half the room had risen to get between him and Travis.

JACKSON

ackson's body ached from when the bitch had beaten him. The hard floor wasn't helping either. Would he ever be able to walk right? It didn't matter. If she had her way, they'd all be dead soon.

"Can you stop glaring at me," Candace said. She sat on the ground across the room with her back against the console, toying idly with the cord of the receiver.

Jackson laughed. "You really need to control everything don't you?"

Candace answered him with her middle finger.

"Classy," he said.

"We're stuck here together. No reason for it not to be pleasant."

"Are you crazy? You've sentenced us all to death and you expect me to be pleasant?"

Candace smiled.

Why the fuck was she smiling?

"I didn't sentence anyone to anything."

"Are you fuckin —" Jackson groaned. If he continued, he'd end up punching her smug face. He took a few deep breaths.

Silence swelled between them as the seconds ticked by.

Jackson scanned the walls, floors, taking in his prison. Or was it his tomb? After he'd inspected it all, he let his eyes drift back to the woman who had doomed them all.

"Not much of a retirement," he said.

Candace seemed confused at first, and then exploded into fits of hysterical laughs. The sound reverberated until it filled every inch of the control room. Jackson couldn't help but smile too.

"No," Candace said. "Not at all. Fuck."

Their laughter ended in wheezes.

Jackson had a hope, a nugget of a plan. "Then why?" he asked, a note of pleading tinged his words. "Why aren't you fighting for a way to fix this?"

Candace watched Jackson for a long time. He didn't see any of the anger or resentment he'd seen before, but in its place was something worse. Pity.

So much time passed that Jackson thought she wasn't going to answer. "Don't you want to see your wife again?" he asked. "I have partners out there who need me. What are they going to think if we never come home?"

"Of course I want to see Julia, but it's not about us," Candace said.

"What? What the fuck does that mean?"

The thing in the hanger slammed against the blast shield again. Jackson flinched at the sudden noise but Candace didn't move. She just turned her head to the spot where the sound had struck.

"Have you ever been to Tali?" she asked

"What?"

"Have you ever been to the capital planet Tali?"

"Yeah. When I was a kid. I went with my parents," Jackson answered, puzzled by the random question.

"Good. Did you go to the Imperial Museum?"

Jackson shook his head. "What does this have to do with anything?"

"I'm getting there. I went with Julia at the end of my last rotation. Used the bonus I got. We stayed in Tali for almost six months. One of the last places we went, when we got tired of the beach, was the Imperial Museum. Did you know they have a map of all the ancient gates? It's more artistic than scientific, but I stood in front of it for half an hour before Julia got fed up with me.

"It was a holo display with thousands of green lights — those are the Zurathel gates — and thin wisps of blue connected them showing the transport lanes. Julia said it looked like a galaxy, but I've always thought it looked like a scan of the brain. The synapses and neurons all lit up."

"What the fuck, Candace? It's a nice story but it has nothing to do with any of this."

"Just let me finish. You wanted to know why we can't try to leave. That map is why. The dead lanes are why. I never used to think about the dead lanes either. No one does. They're exceedingly rare, and we don't really understand how the gates work. I saw those dead lanes on that map and did some research. 'The gate just got knocked out of their gravitational plane' or 'it suddenly just stopped working.' That's what the Empire says. It's unfortunate, sure, but not really interesting in the grand scheme." She paused as the monster pounded on the blast shield over and over.

God it must be massive, Jackson thought.

When it ceased, Candace continued. "I was stationed on Brondine a few years into my career when the lane between it and Traxa went dead. We were waiting for a transmission and right before it was time, we got a massive energy spike. Lit the control panel up. Sparks everywhere.

Crew came in and said the modulation banks malfunctioned. They fixed them, but we never got contact from Traxa again. That's when they said the lane was dead. Which sucks for Traxa and for Zurathel Corp, but Traxa are a sustainable planet, and they weren't a main line. So they'll be fine. They have their own means of production and the Empire sent a commission out to reestablish the net for them. Though, even in the fastest ship it will take eleven hundred years for them to get there. But I'm thinking about the eight billion people on Traxa cut off from the rest of the Empire. From the network. What will they tell the rest of the Empire when they can finally communicate with us?"

Jackson thought he was starting to understand. He licked his lips and shifted uncomfortably.

"Then I thought about today. What if while we were here feeling the quacking, Vexel saw a massive power spike? Like I did all those years ago. The Empire has been to the gates of other dead lanes. They lay out relays in space and reestablish the network. But we never hear from those planets. It can take decades or centuries between when the lane goes dead and a connection reestablished. Everyone who would care is already dead. The Empire doesn't even report it to the media."

"I know what you're getting at, and you're wrong. If this has happened before, we would know about it. There'd be protocols for it." Jackson's voice was barely more than a whisper.

"Would we? Do you really think they would tell us? There are thousands of gates on as many planets connecting us across the universe in a way we could never match under any other means. All of the Empire relies on the gates. The Empire wouldn't risk everything by telling the public the truth."

"Someone would talk. Something like that couldn't stay quiet forever."

"Maybe," she said. "There have only been fifty-two dead lanes in the whole of Empire history. What are fifty-two planets and a few billion lives against the rest of the Empire? Truly think about it. Why have a deadlock switch at all if nothing like this can happen? Why keep it hardwired in and not just have the control added to our clips? The more you look at it, the more you start to see that none of this makes sense."

Candace pulled herself up to her feet and nimbly walked over to a cabinet in the wall, placed her empty water bottle in it, and pressed the fill button.

Jackson watched as his heart hammered in his chest. It beat so fast that dizziness began to take over him.

When the bottle was filled, Candace drank it empty, refilled it, then walked back to her spot and sat down.

"So yeah," she said. "I don't think they're sending help." The corners of her lips lifted into a weak smile. "I'm sure Julia and the rest of our loved ones will get some made up story about what happened to us. Solar flare cooked the planet and destroyed the outpost. Knocked the gate out of alignment. Just another dead lane. They'll pay out our contracts to them and the death benefits, too. Julia will survive. They'll all move on. They'll be safe."

Candace wiped away the tears falling down her cheeks and sniffed. "The worst part is that they are right to do it."

"You can't mean that. We don't know anything about that thing out there. Let me get to the armory and kill it."

Candace chuckled through her tears. "You want to shoot bullets at a thing that survived an explosion powerful enough to destroy an ancient, indestructible gate? Come on Jackson. *Think.* This is what it means to be in charge. You have to be willing to make the decisions that are hard, but right. If this has happened before and the Empire knows about it, then why haven't we ever heard from the planets that were dead laned? 'Cause everyone there is dead. And if the Empire does know about it, there will be no rescue team because they can't risk that thing getting out. They'll just disconnect access to the gate to keep it contained."

"But —" Jackson sighed. What else could he say? Candace didn't understand. Worse, she was crazy. If she wanted him to start acting like a leader then he would, and his first act was to end this fucking quarantine. The monster could stay in the hangar until they knew how to deal with it, but he was going to get the rest of the survivors out of the rec room. Once they got here, they could figure out what to do together, and if Candace wanted to stay, then so be it. This was her fault after all.

The conversation lapsed back into silence. In his current state,

Jackson wasn't sure if he could beat her in a fight if she tried to stop him from enacting his slowly-forming plan. It was hard enough to sit. If he had to stand and fight he would probably end up on the ground again. Hours slinked by.

Jackson was starting to lose his mind so he began to contemplate his escape. It was simple: wait for Candace to fall asleep, get to the control panel to re-atmosphere the outpost, open all the doors. He hoped Candace wouldn't reverse it. Jackson didn't think she would be that heartless.

So he sat and watched Candace on the other side of the room. She dozed with her back against one end of the console and the long piece of metal resting on her lap.

He needed to end the quarantine protocol, but he didn't know how. *We rely way too much on these fucking discs in the back of our necks. Why didn't they teach us this in training?* He could clearly imagine Candace's response if he'd asked her: "Because they don't want us to know. They want us to die." Well, fuck that.

When Jackson got back to Virgo or Vexel-7, he would make sure that all operations commanders knew how to fully operate any outpost without their clip. But first, he had to figure out how to get past the bitch without waking her up.

His stomach was cramped with hunger, his bladder was achingly full, and his balls felt like they were swollen to the size of oranges.

Jackson contemplated the consequences of urinating in the corner as he stood. His knees groaned and popped. Pain flared. He sucked in through his teeth and tasted the stale human flavor of the room. Keeping an eye on Candace, he inched forward. Her chest rose and fell rhythmically, her eyes moved quickly behind her eyelids. Jackson stopped after each step, waiting for Candace's eyes to pop open and for her to jump to her feet and attack him.

Step. *Pause.* Step. *Pause.* Step. *Pause.*

When Jackson reached the control panel, he froze. All of the nobs, buttons, dials, and plastic sliders made no sense to him. If they had ever been labeled, those markings had long since faded away. Any of them — or all of them — could be used to reset the outpost security systems. He flipped a switch and behind him, one of the monitors blinked to life. On it Jackson could see the camera feed of the hangar on the other side of the blast doors. It was a miracle the camera still worked at all.

The Avealus Gate drew his eye first. It was a mess. Cracked and pitted. Giant chunks were knocked out of the arch, jutting out at strange angles and only holding on by some strange strength of will, leaving it appearing more like a strange abstract piece of art than the ancient archway it had been. As Jackson studied the structure, he could clearly see several of the long cracks running through it slowly pulling back together.

Jackson began to hope. If this continued, the gate might soon be whole and healed. His spirits lifted and he began to scan the room for the monster or any other threat that would prevent him from reaching the gate and getting it back online.

The floor was a battlefield. The concrete slabs pointed out in odd ways. Bodies and limbs were strewn everywhere. Blood painted every surface. His hand gripped at his chest. He wanted to crumble. To cry. So much senseless death. He had to force himself to keep taking it in, but he never saw a monster. There was a moment where he thought he had, but when he looked closer, there was nothing there. Jackson shrugged it off as a glitch in the camera or trick of the eye. No monster was visible on the screen. Where the hell did it go? His temper spiked. That whole speech of hers had almost had him convinced that their situation was hopeless. Now he knew better.

"Fuck you," Jackson whispered.

Something moved beside him. He caught it on the edges of his periphery. He turned his head in time to see the pipe as it flew at him. It connected just above his left temple. Searing pain ripped through him. Blood gushed down the side of his face, soaking his shirt and splattering onto the console controls. He stumbled backwards, fighting to stay on his feet. He barely registered the next strike. The pipe bashed the front of his face, shattering his teeth.

The world lurched as he crumpled to the floor, choking on bits of broken teeth. The last thing he saw was the livid expression on Candace's face as she raised the bloodied rod for another blow.

JARED

ared never considered himself to be a lucky person. He was working sanitation on a speck of a rock hidden in deep space, cleaning up after messy, nasty people of over twenty-five hundred different species. Making sure they had a clean place to wait while they traveled to somewhere important. It wasn't hard work. Outpost 9106 was so rarely used, there wasn't even a whole lot of it to do, but it was still a shitty job. Everyone else who had "important" jobs looked down on the sanitation guys. That was okay. It was easy enough to take a piss in the filtered water tank and watch as the fuckers took a drink of it.

Today, Jared wasn't sure if his luck had gotten worse or better. When the explosion occurred, he had been in the atmospheric room smoking a cigarette. It was his little hideaway. There were no cameras there, and no one else ever went in unless they were exchanging the tanks.

The impact of the explosion had sent him rocking back against pipes. A moment later the machinery that handled the atmospheric conditioning of the outpost kicked on, sucking in gasses instead of pumping them out. There was only one reason for the inflows to be used in a moment like that. They had entered quarantine, and Jared knew enough not to get caught in the vacuum. He cursed and grabbed his plastic helmet and snapped it on, hearing the familiar hiss as his suit pressurized. He breathed a sigh of relief.

How many of the other workers hadn't been as lucky as him to have a cleaning suit on? He didn't want to think of that. There were people out there he kinda liked, well . . . liked well enough not to wish for their deaths. That was a thought for a different time. Now he needed to figure out what was going on.

The atmo room was not a place to get stuck in during quarantine. There was no food, no water system, nothing. He might be dead before anyone thought to even check for him. He tried to call the control room, but no one answered. He flicked his eye to pull up the messenger system on his clip but nothing happened. That was when he noticed the entire HUD was gone. Panicking, he ran to the door and tried to lift it open but it wouldn't budge. Deep down Jared knew it wouldn't. The quarantine protocol would magnetize the doors to maintain and guarantee they stayed sealed shut. Regardless, he pounded on the door and shouted for help, but his fists and his voice made no noise in the still void around him. After a time, he stumbled, defeated to spot along the wall and slunk to the ground to wait for the quarantine to end.

Hours passed. It was hard to track without the clock on the clip. Jared whiled away the time by chatting empty things with himself.

Why was this quarantine taking so long? He'd been stuck in a lockdown ten years earlier. It had only lasted two hours. Some idiot had crossed the gate carrying a weird disease. The sensors registered the unknown pathogen, analyzed it, and discovered that it was resistant to the normal cleaning systems, so the quarantine crew stormed in and sanitized the hangar, the vents, the halls. All in two hours. The longest part was doling out vaccines and treatments to crew and guests holed up in the locked and pressurized rooms. So what the hell had happened here? With the Clip gone he guessed it had been twelve hours already. After that long in the suit, claustrophobia was setting in and he didn't know how much breathable air he had left. But time was running low.

Jared pushed at the door leading out into the hangar corridor, but it wouldn't budge. He kicked, punched, and shouted at it. Panic set in. He was too big to squeeze in the vents. The giant gas tanks couldn't help him unless he wanted to open one of the valves, light his lighter and blow the whole room up. Then Jared had a thought: Every room had a hatch in the floor leading the maintenance tunnels. The hatches were designed to be opened electronically but he could probably force it open with enough effort.

He went over to the hatch at the other end of the room. After a few minutes of work with his belt knife, he managed to get the blade underneath the tile that disguised the hatch door and lift the hatch open.

The tile swung open revealing a black hole. Jared pulled out his flashlight and shined it into the pit. The hole held nothing more than a metal ladder descending through a concrete tube. The shadows drank the light. He couldn't see more than a few feet down. *Fuck,* he thought and began his descent.

The door shut itself behind him with a soft *thunk,* plunging the tunnel into silence and darkness. A sudden shadow shocked him and the flashlight slipped from his plastic covered hand and fell forever until it landed with a smack on the floor below. Echoes reverberated in every direction and Jared waited quietly for some response. None came.

With nowhere to go but onward, Jared followed after it. The ting of boot on metal as he stepped on each rung and crinkle of his thin plastic suit were the only sounds in the dark abyss. The tube was tight. It constricted him on all sides. He hated small spaces even when times were normal. When the tube ended and the ladder opened up into cavernous maintenance tunnels, Jared could feel the wide open space even though he couldn't see it. In a vacuum he shouldn't have been able to. Maybe it was just the weight of the darkness lessening.

The maintenance tunnels were rarely used for anything more than the storage of spare oxygen tanks, cleaning supplies, and equipment for the maintenance crew. They had originally been created to allow the maintenance staff to be able to quickly reach any part of an outpost without being seen by the people who were living there and to fix things like the plumbing and electrical without anyone knowing they were doing it, but with so little traffic at this Outpost, it just wasn't necessary to stay out of sight, so Jared rarely used these tunnels.

Jared knew he'd reached the bottom of the ladder when his heel crunched on the broken glass of the flashlights lens.

In appearance the tunnels were the opposite of the layout above them. Where the main level was designed like a grid: large, cubed rooms with small halls in between them, the maintenance tunnels were wide open spaces with thin pillars to hold it all up.

"Where to now?" he asked the empty tunnels. The only answer that occurred to him was the kitchens. He didn't know where the others were, but the kitchen would have food, water, and wouldn't be depressurized. He took a step to the left then hesitated. In the dark, he couldn't read the name plates on the ladders. The kitchens were to the left, he knew that much, but how far? He counted the rooms above from memory. After the atmo room there was the equipment room and then the kitchens and then the main waiting area. So two ladders.

Breathing slowly he felt his way forward in the dark using his feet to check for obstructions until he reached the second ladder. Jared didn't hesitate when he began to climb. The thought of food and freedom from the confining suit propelled him upward.

At the top he paused. A thin sliver of light leaked through a gap in the hatch. He swore. Had the explosion trashed the kitchen and knocked the hatch off its hinges? With both hands he pushed. The hatch door protested but eventually he got it all the way open and he lifted himself through.

The room was different. The gray stone of the room was the same as every other. It took him a moment to realize that the debris scattered everywhere was from the tables and chairs of the human visitor waiting room. Mixed with the metal and plastic detritus was the dust and brick from the wall. The doorway was gone. Only a jagged, gaping hole remained.

"Fuck," he said. "What in all that is holy happened here?"

As Jared turned to head back down the hatch, something moved in the hallway. Steadily, the sound of heavy, fleshy footsteps drew closer. Then they were in the room with him. But he couldn't see anything.

A sharp, eye-bleeding sound pierced his mind. The buzzing made it hard to think. A pile of broken debris suddenly scattered as if it had been brushed aside. But there was no one there.

Jared jumped backward, tripped over a stray stone, and fell onto a pile of broken chairs. Bright flowers of pain bloomed across his arms, back, and chest. His heart nearly stopped when he heard the suit tear. Air exploded out of it before he was able to clasp his hand over the hole.

The invisible thing stopped moving. Jared watched, gasping in pain and terror. The plastic over his face fogged as his hot breath escaped him in gulps. In his head, the buzzing turned into a shriek.

"What are you?"

The shrieking gave the being form in his mind. He could see the beauty of it, and the horror. What it was, where it was coming from, was suddenly evident to him. He didn't want it, and yet he wanted nothing else. The creature turned its head and creeped closer to Jared. His instincts told him to run. To dive down the hatch. But he couldn't move.

The monster shrieked and slammed the hatch down with a bang.

TRAVIS

t took three days for Travis to turn Devon's idea into a reality. He and Devon had expected it to be a simple procedure, but neither of them had understood just how complex the clip was.

Aeon had been a major hindrance to their progress. He had yelled, threatened, and stormed at them, but as the hours ticked by and turned to days, he and the others in the rec room began to believe that they would never make it happen. Even Devon had told Travis he didn't think it was possible anymore.

Travis plowed on though. His mind needed a problem to chew on, and his heart needed the hope this problem provided. Hunger, panic, and despair had taken root in the room but Travis would not let it destroy him too.

On the third day, Travis began to understand something he hadn't before: just how lazy bureaucracy was. Instead of replacing old systems with new ones, they just added on the new like layers of paint, leaving the old systems behind to be forgotten. If he got out of this, he'd find the person who'd made that decision and kiss them. Their laziness may just save everyone's lives.

Travis separated out the wires from the door panel, pulling

out two blue and green ones. They were from before, when the whole outpost was hardwired into its own internal network and controlled via tablet computers. Twisting them together, he connected those wires to the ones he'd attached to his clip. Sparks arced and burned his arm.

"Flipping fudger," he cursed, sucking on a tingling fingertip.

Rita grabbed his shoulder and spun him around. "Are you alright?" she asked, looking him over clinically. Devon stepped closer.

Travis ignored them both. His clip had come back on. It did not begin its bootup sequence like it had been newly installed, but brought up the last page he had been on.

"Ha!" he shouted with glee.

The pool cue from their game earlier hung in the air in front of him. Travis closed the game and smiled for the first time in days. Hope, real hope, swelled in his chest. He reached behind his neck and yanked the blue and green wires out from the clip. Now that it was synced with the internal network, he wouldn't need them. Travis reattached the plate that covered the clip's inner mechanism and then put the camera drone back on top.

"Did you get it?" Rita asked. Her voice was hushed and urgent. She kept stealing glances over her shoulder toward Aeon, who stood back with his arms crossed over his chest.

"Let's see," Travis said, still smiling. He blinked twice and brought up the main system menu then scrolled through submenus and options. Whoever had programmed the outpost had done a good job of hiding the override systems, but at last he found them. Now, all that was left was to hope he had the necessary permissions.

Travis turned his head towards the door and saw the prompt to open it appear in his vision. He hesitated. What if it didn't open? What if it opened, but wouldn't close again? There were so many problems that could arise, so many dangers: disease, radiation, intruders. *Should I do this?* Travis turned to ask Rita and saw Aeon standing not far away, venom in his eyes. The sight of him was all Travis needed. He turned back to the door and pressed the button in his mind.

The door hissed open. The force of the air rushing out of the room yanked him toward the door. He grabbed the doorway and pushed himself back. The 'Close' prompt hung in the air before him, and he pressed it, sending the door back down like the blade of a guillotine.

Travis shouted in triumph. The sound of his voice was lost in a deluge of noise that was a mixture of joy and outrage as the crowd roused behind him. He turned back to Devon and Rita and was met by a sea of bodies all speaking at once, some to him, some to their neighbors, no clear consensus on their faces.

"Shut up!" Aeon shouted over the tumult. He had to bark twice more before the talking began to die down.

Travis found Aeon's face in the crowd and their eyes met.

"What the fuck do you think you're doing?" Aeon shouted. "You could have killed us all. That was air we need."

"You already know that isn't true," Rita said before Travis could respond. "Your friend was the one to explain how every room has its own independent air supply pumped in. So why don't you do what you said and shut up. I'm tired of hearing you."

The crowd nodded in agreement. There was muttering of shut ups and sit downs scattered in. Hunger, panic, and despair had set in, but it hadn't yet sunk in so deep that common sense had gone out the proverbial window.

Aeon took two steps towards them before his own group pulled him back.

"Okay," Travis said loudly to the crowd that had gotten to its feet. "Nothing about the plan has changed. I'm gonna head out of here and make my way to the gate. I'm just gonna try and figure out what state it's in and see if I can get it working. Barring that, I'm gonna try and get the net up and running."

"We," Devon said.

Travis glared at him. Devon glared back. They had agreed

that Devon would stay here. They had argued about it for hours, and Devon had said that he understood.

"I know we talked about it, and I know I agreed to stay, but I was lying. I'm coming and you can't stop me."

"Fine," Travis said.

Travis turned back to the crowd. Scared and anxious faces gazed back at him. "I walked Rita through how to plug in to the speaker system, so Devon and I will be able to keep in touch and give you regular updates. And you all can let us know if something happens here, too."

He paused and waited for someone to ask a question. People nodded, but no one spoke up.

"You aren't all buying this?" Aeon shouted. "It's obvious what they're doing. They're just gonna —"

"Seriously, shut up," someone else shouted back. Travis was grateful for the support, but didn't like the desperate rage he saw on Aeon's face. He and Devon needed to leave now before Aeon did something drastic.

Agalla, please keep us in your heart, Travis prayed. *Let your power grant us strength and your grace grant us calm in these troubled times.* "I think I may visit a temple or two if we ever get back to civilization," Travis said. He smiled at Devon, and the love of his life smiled back.

"I didn't take you as religious?" Devon said.

"I'm not, but my parents were. I think I may take it up if we make it out of this."

"We will. I have faith in you."

Aeon snorted and scowled. Travis began to tell him to 'fudge off' but stopped when Devon squeezed his arm. At first, he thought it was out of caution, but that wasn't what Travis saw in Devon's eyes. What he saw was fear.

Travis forced another smile to try and calm his partner before approaching the doorway.

"Thanks," he said. "Ready?"

Devon nodded and turned to face the door. They both stepped up to it, their shoes hitting the metal.

"Remember to push out all the air you possibly can. We will go as long as we can and then duck into a room for more air. The living quarters should all be pressurized. And don't forget to follow me. It's right first, then the first left."

Devon nodded. Travis blinked and saw the door command pop up. He was about to click it when a hand gripped his elbow.

"Be careful," Rita said.

Travis peered out into the crowd and lingered on Aeon, who radiated murder. "You too," he said.

She let go and backed away from the door. Then, Travis and Devon both pushed all of the air from their lungs. It made his chest ache and burn instantly, but he didn't have time to second guess the decision. He clicked the icon and the door sprang up.

Travis and Devon were sucked into the hall. As soon as he had his footing, Travis ordered the door shut. He found it hard to do over the pressure in his skull and the burning of his chest. As the door closed, Travis spared one last glance for the rec room, certain he was about to die.

AEON

eon had had enough of this. Three days of the traitors' plots and lies was enough to drive anyone insane, and he was going to put a stop to it.

"They got twenty minutes then I'm going after them," he said. He walked up to the door and turned and reiterated it to the whole room. A chorus of shouts rebounded on him, but not as many as the traitors would have expected. Their only way out of this room had just left, and Aeon knew that the remaining people understood that. Now all he needed to do was amp that up, and when he gave them another way out, they'd follow him.

Rita backed away.

Three steps brought him to her, and he whispered, "You're gonna show me how they opened the door, and you're gonna do it now." He didn't bother to hide the threat in his tone.

"I don't know how," she said.

With grim satisfaction he watched the color drain from her face. "Yes, you do. You sat with that traitor the whole time. Watched the whole thing. Now you're gonna do it for me. If you don't, well —" His voice trailed off as he cracked his knuckles.

"Do what you're gonna do then. Beat me, kill me, whatever,

but it won't get you what you want. I'm a doctor not an engineer. I can't help you."

Aeon was ready to do what she asked. The only thing that stopped him was the crowd. If he hurt her now, that would turn them against him for good, and he couldn't have that.

"Fine," he said with a smile. "Just remember that your only friends left you here with me, and I'm gonna get out of here one way or another. You should consider what condition you want to be in when I do."

DEVON

Devon knew he shouldn't have come. Slim as he was, he was not an athletic man and his lungs were not built for this. His chest burned and ached, nearly on the verge of collapse. Worse was the silence, the utter silence of the dark, empty hallway. No, it was not okay. How could someone handle a quiet like this?

They reached the first branch and Travis turned left. They were halfway to the first door when Travis began to slow. It caught him off guard, and Devon nearly toppled into him. Devon wanted to ask what was wrong but as he got closer, he saw past Travis and understood. Six of their friends and coworkers lay dead in the hall, bottlenecked outside the doorway. Quarantine locked out as well as in, and they had died because of it. He hoped it was a quick death.

Travis pushed one corpse out of the way, revealing half of another, and opened the door. They stumbled in, and Travis shut it.

Air flooded back into their lungs. To Devon, it was like the first bit of water after having been lost in the desert. His head swam. He didn't even mind the smell of death, the way it made the air smell like an unclean toilet. He was just happy they had made it this far and allowed himself to hope. The gate wasn't much further. If this was the worst of it, they really would be able to make it out alive.

At least that was what he thought. He didn't know how wrong he was.

CANDACE

andace stared at the monitors with a blank expression on her face. After three days, the buzzing in her skull had grown so loud and so persistent she didn't even notice it anymore. It wanted inside her head. How she knew that, she couldn't say, but she did. The only thing keeping it from rooting into her more deeply was the wall of stone, metal, and glass between her and the hangar. These things had looked so insurmountable when the explosion had happened. They seemed feeble now. A paper shield.

She accepted the pain and violation of it all. After she'd moved Jackson's body to a corner of the room, she'd scoured the camera feeds and counted the dead. There were eight crew and one hundred and three guests. One hundred and eleven dead, all because of her. What was a little pain as payment? Soon there would be another fifty to add to her count. Candace wondered if she would still be alive to watch the last of them die. She hoped she was. She deserved to have to bear witness to their suffering.

Why didn't I just flip the fucking deadlock? If I had, they would all be alive and I would be at home with Julia.

Candace allowed herself to cry. Without Jackson to hold her

back, she let down the walls she'd built up inside herself. Grief, shame, despair, rage, all came flooding in. She drowned in them for hours, curled up on the floor, cursing at the empty air around her. She drifted in and out of sleep, and eventually the darkness passed, not slowly or gradually, but all at once. After a while, she dragged the remaining chair back to the console and began relearning the manual controls for the outpost.

She scanned the different camera feeds searching for the monster that decimated the hangar. She wanted to stop, but couldn't bring herself to do it.

It happened the third day after the explosion. Candace was staring at the screen watching her coworkers in the rec room. Travis and Devon had been trying in vain to open the door, and even that had grown tedious as the days passed, yet she kept watching.

The monster slammed on the metal blast door behind her. Shocked, Candace fell out of her chair and onto the floor. The buzzing in her skull amplified to a low pitched howl.

A part of her had hoped the thing had died, but now that it was active again, her curiosity compelled her to see if she could find out what it was doing. She cycled through the different camera feeds until she found the hangar. The monster was among a pile of corpses, peeling off the flesh of the dead and wrapping its invisible body in them. She gagged then vomited.

Candace turned the feed to a different camera, trying to block out the image of the surgical-like cuts the monster had made on the carcasses. Why was it doing that? Why now after all these days? She thought she understood why. With an effort, she turned the feed back to the hangar. The Avealus Gate was nearly whole and restored. The black field in the inside of the arch was still absent — and maybe the dampeners would keep it that way — but there was no way to know for sure if the gate could magically heal itself.

A face passed near the camera. Then another, and another. Faces attached to necks that stretched for a dozen feet or more, with empty eyes looking at her looking at them. They stared at each other for a long time before Candace found the strength to change the feed. She recommenced her mad cycling of the cameras when movement on the screen made her stop.

There were people out in the hallway. Two men ran through the halls. It was Travis and Devon, but what they were doing, and how they had done it? She watched as they sprinted down one hall and then another before nearly falling when they came upon the pile of corpses. They stopped and Travis kicked one body aside and then somehow opened another door.

What do you think you're doing?

Frantically she searched around for the call box. She needed to tell them to stop. Then she remembered that her clip was still connected to it, and she didn't need the call box anymore. Her only fear was that Travis wouldn't be able to hear her since he was no longer in the rec room.

"Travis?" she asked. *Please respond. You have no idea how dangerous things are. You have to know. You have to understand.* Only silence answered her. Was he ignoring her or could he not respond? Did it matter? If he was going to the gate, if he turned it back on, billions would die. She couldn't let that happen. What if he could fix it or turn it back on from a distance? He might not even have to get past the monster. She *wouldn't* let it happen.

Her hand drifted to the room controls. With a few flips of a switch she could vent the air from their room and end this now. What were two more dead in the grand scheme? They would die anyway. If they didn't starve or suffocate in the halls, the monster would rip them apart if they entered the hangar.

Push it. Her hand shook, only millimeters away. A brush of her hand. A flick of her fingers and her *problems* would be gone. But she couldn't. There was a difference between letting it happen and doing it yourself, she discovered, and she couldn't do it herself. Not yet.

"Travis," she said again. "If you can still hear me, please answer. Trav —"

TRAVIS

"Travis say something."

Travis heard Candace but didn't respond. There was nothing to say to her. Nothing constructive, at least. If she was content to let everyone die, then that was on her. Her authority didn't matter anymore. He sat on the bed in the unused living quarters with his knees tucked to his chest while Devon cried silently a few feet away. What could Travis say or do to make any of this right? Devon didn't want to hear Travis's plan or his offers of condolences, and for the first time, he understood the divide between the types of people they were. Travis was devastated by the death outside their room, but he'd never gotten to know any of the dead. They were just faces to him. It wasn't the same for Devon, and Travis didn't know which was worse: Was it better to love like that and be flattened by loss or was it better to keep your distance?

"Travis, if you can hear me please wave to the camera," Candace repeated.

Above him in the corner, Travis found the camera, a small glossy black eye watching them. They were supposed to be deactivated when a living quarter was occupied but maybe the quarantine protocol overrode that? It made sense to Travis. The

rescue team would need to know where to find the survivors —
and the dead.

"Travis?"

Why was she reaching out to him now? It had been three
days of no contact. Was it just the fact that they were on the
move, or had something happened?

"What?" he asked.

"What are you doing?"

Travis ground his teeth. "You know what, Candace. Stop
playing stupid."

There was a long pause. Devon had stopped crying, and their
eyes met. He pressed his index finger to his lips and mouthed
the word 'quiet'. Anger flared in Travis like a summer storm
melting his fear and exhaustion.

Just when he was sure she wouldn't speak again, Candace
responded. "You have to stop," she said. "You don't understand
what you are risking."

"Stop playing. You've had days to fill us all in on what is
going on, but you've said nothing. You left us all to die.
Slowly. I'm done listening to you. We're going, and you can't
stop us."

Another long pause.

Travis stood up. He wrapped himself in his rage, gripping it
like a life jacket.

"Come on," he said to Devon. "Let's keep moving. I can't
stand the smell in here."

Devon sighed in relief. They left the bedchamber and
skidded across the blood-soaked floor to the door.

"Please stop," Candace pleaded. "There is a monster in the
outpost with us. It's what destroyed the gate. Left it in pieces.
You can't fix it."

"Then why do you care if we try?" Travis asked.

"I saw what it did to the guests, Travis. I won't let that
happen to the rest of us."

Travis rested his head against the cool stone wall of the

sitting room and shut his eyes. What was she on that she thought he'd believe that?

"Put Jackson on," he said. "Let him confirm this monster thing. It's long past time you stepped down anyway. You are clearly unfit to be in charge."

There was another long pause.

Good. Let her try and force him to lie.

"I can't," she said.

"What is she saying?" Devon asked. "What's going on?"

Travis growled and punched the wall. "Can't or won't?" he asked Candace. "You know what? It doesn't matter. Take your attachment out of the box and put his in."

"I told you I can't." Candace sighed. "He's dead."

Travis blinked.

"What? How? We heard him earlier."

Travis held his breath while he waited for the answer.

"He —"

Travis could hear the pain in her voice. The sound dulled the edge of his anger.

"He got hurt in the blast. I didn't think it was too bad, but he went to sleep and didn't wake up."

Travis cut the connection. "Fuck."

"What?" Devon asked. "What did she say?"

It was so convenient. *Too convenient.* Was Jackson really dead? Or was she lying and keeping him from talking? If he was dead, it was entirely her fault. Both Sally and Jackson could have been saved in the med bay, but by enforcing this stupid lockdown, she had sentenced both of them to death. *Why, though?* It didn't make sense. None of this made any sense. If a rescue wasn't coming, why stop them from trying to save themselves?

Candace sighed. "I know how it sounds —"

"Do you? You're sentencing fifty people to death, and all for what, to keep some monster from killing us?"

Travis began to ask Devon if he could make any more sense of this than he could, but then remembered that Devon couldn't hear Candace's side of the conversation. He wished he was back in the rec room so that everyone could hear this and weigh in.

"It's not just that," Candace said. "It's not just what it would do to us, but everyone else too."

"Everyone who?" Travis asked. "Are there other people here?"

"Will you talk to me?" Devon asked.

Travis shushed him with a wave of his hand and began to speak but Candace cut in.

"Come to the control room. I'll show you everything. I'll even atmo the halls so you can breathe."

The connection ended. Travis severed his too. She might be able to see them, but he wouldn't let her hear them too.

"She wants me to come to the control room. You should head back to the rec room so I can keep everyone in the loop."

Devon shook his head. "Hell no. I'm going where you go."

Travis was ready to argue, but he knew better. He sighed. There was no point in engaging Devon's stubborn streak more than he already had.

"Fine. But we are stopping to get suits on the way. I'm not getting trapped in a hall if she decides to vent them on us."

Devon nodded and smiled.

"We go slow. You hear the vents scrape, expel the air in your lungs and pop into the closest room. Got it?"

CANDACE

andace flipped the switch. The vents ground to life, and oxygen flooded the hangar and halls. Then she walked to the far end of the console and flipped another. This broke the magnetic locks on all of the doors, ending the quarantine completely. It hadn't even been that hard. Once she'd started to understand the layout of the control panel it had been easy to guess which switches did what.

"That's it then," she said, leaning heavily on the metal console and staring through the hangar window.

She lifted the blast shield. There was no longer any reason to keep it down. If the monster wanted to break into the control room, she would let it. Her fate wouldn't be any different than the others.

She sensed the monster in the hangar, like it was waiting for something. She scanned the hangar for the monster and saw it hanging from the ceiling like a fleshy many-faced spider.

Across from it, the gate continued to heal. Was that what the monster was waiting for? A way out? Somehow she knew that that was it. A voice, maybe the monster's, told her so. The voice mingled with a strong sense of hunger and deep patience that made every inch of her body tingle.

It was wrong. She'd never experienced real evil before, but it was the only word that seemed to match the feelings emanating from the creature in that hangar. She couldn't let it escape. No cost would be too high to keep it from leaving. If souls existed, she understood that hers was damned for what she'd done and what she had to do, but it didn't matter. It was her mistake to rectify. She only wished that others didn't have to pay the price along with her.

Her fingers trembled as she reached the final switch. If she flipped it, there would be no going back. She would truly be a murderer. *You already are. What was it that you did to Jackson if not murder?*

A silent shape moved out of the hole that had been the door to the waiting area. It moved across the hangar and towards the door she intended to open. So there was a second one, one that was still invisible? The only mark of its passing were a few red footprints on the clean brick. Did it know what she was planning? How could it?

Candace held her breath and closed her eyes then flipped the switch. The door slid open. Guilt bloomed in the pit of her stomach as bloody footsteps appeared and the invisible monster slipped out into the halls of Outpost 9106.

"I'm sorry guys. Please forgive me," she whispered then began to cry. While she cried, one-hundred and three cold faces, one-hundred and three pairs of pitless eyes watched her from high above.

Patient the monster that remained, hanging motionless from the ceiling, watched, and waited for what would come next.

TRAVIS

The air was already pressurized when Travis opened the door. There was no rush of air out into the hall. No push. Travis thought he might hold tight on his promise to visit the temples and offer thanks to the gods if their luck kept turning around. Nevertheless, he still moved cautiously down the hallway. Some buried instinct told him not to trust Candace.

Devon bounced along behind him, his hand clenched around Travis's arm. He seemed almost buoyant. Thankfully, he listened well and didn't talk.

Despite being fresh, the air in the halls seemed stale, and no matter how far away they got, Travis could still smell the reek of the dead. They turned left, then right, then left again. He wasn't sure if they were going in the right direction. The outpost was so much larger than he thought. He had only ever visited a small portion of the five hundred living quarters, and a few of the other rooms.

The suits were in the maintenance locker room which was in the top corner, away from the rec room and opposite the control room. There was no straight shot to either from where they were, and the presence of the labs and med bay threw him off, causing him to backtrack and circle around. He wasn't sure they would have been able to make it without the air back in the halls. They paused at a junction.

"What's that noise?" Devon asked.

Travis stopped and listened, but he didn't hear anything. Devon leaned against the wall and pressed the heel of his palm into his eyes.

"There's nothing," Travis said and began walking, but Devon grabbed his arm and pulled him back. Travis saw his bright blue eyes, ghostly and afraid in the dim light.

"You can't hear the buzzing?"

Travis squeezed Devon's shoulder. "It's just the stress," he said. For a moment he thought he could hear it — a faint and barely audible hum — but brushed it off as just the noise of the lights above them.

Devon's head twitched and his eyes shut.

"Come on," Travis said. "I don't like us out in the open like this. Let's get to the suits."

"Okay. God, you can't hear that?"

"Move," Travis urged. The buzz was louder, but it wasn't important, their mission was what mattered.

Click click click click. Click click click click.

At the next junction they stopped. The halls were empty in every direction, but Travis sensed he was being watched. Candace, he told himself, just Candace.

Click click click click. Click click click click.

What was that noise? It sounded like metal on rock, and there were a lot of them, like a baby's rattle. When had it started? Where was it coming from? What was making it?

He glanced down each hallway and saw nothing in any direction. The clicking was coming from the left. *Closer. Closer.* He could feel a pressure on the back of his mind weighing him down and urging him to stop. Was this the monster Candace had mentioned?

"It doesn't sound close," Travis said in a voice barely above a whisper.

Devon shrugged and swallowed. "Maybe we should go a little faster? In case Candace is right, and there actually is something in the outpost with us."

"Yeah," Travis agreed. "But stay quiet."

They turned right, and began to move faster. The sound of their footsteps grew louder the quicker they went. And so did the clicking. Faster and closer. *What the hell is following us?* A glance over his shoulder revealed nothing, but in his mind Travis saw long talons and sharp teeth.

Left, straight, right. Panic pushed them forward. The clicking drew closer still, until it was almost on top of them. Travis put his hand out, stopping Devon in his tracks. They were close to the locker room. Travis glimpsed something to his right, halfway down a dead-end hall. He turned to Devon to tell him and gasped. Devon was bleeding from his nose and ears. He didn't seem to notice, or if he did, he didn't care.

"Hey, you're —"

A sound like steel sheets being torn apart roared through the halls. It clawed at his ears, at his brain. Travis looked for the origin of the screech. He thought it came from the left of them, but with the way it bounced off the walls, it could have easily come from anywhere. They couldn't stay in the open like this.

Then he saw it. Or thought he did. Something was down the hall to the left of them. Watching them. He still couldn't *see* it, but he could feel it boring a hole into his brain.

"Move," Travis shouted and shoved Devon toward the locker room door. "Run."

"You first," Devon said.

Travis saw the maintenance locker room door and commanded it to open.

The door is only twenty feet away. Just twenty feet. We can make it.

"Go, so I can shut the door behind us." He shoved Devon again then followed. Behind him, the thing sprang forward. He could hear its heavy steps as it ran toward them, closing the distance.

"Faster," Travis shouted. His word cracked like a whip and Devon sprinted.

Ten feet. *Just a little further.*

Nine feet.

Five.

When they were four feet away, Travis pushed Devon through the door. The shove threw Travis off balance. He stumbled and missed the door slamming into the frame. Travis bounced off the cold metal and tumbled to the floor.

The monster lunged at him the moment he fell. Its claws whispered along his back as it flew over him, slicing fabric and flesh alike in long lines across his skin. A rush of air, hot and acrid, wafted over him. A thud boomed out as the thing collided with the wall at the end of the hall leaving deep cracks in the stone. Pain. Searing, inhuman pain scorched along his back where its claws had grazed him.

A yowl burst from Travis's lips as he scrambled to his feet. Metal squealed as long gouges formed on the floor a few feet from him. Travis shrieked in panic and pain and threw himself through the doorway frantically bringing up the command to shut the door. The thing bashed into the door just as it shut.

Travis heaved and groaned on the floor. The room sweltered, and his back burned where the thing had gouged him.

"Travis. Travis. What's wrong?" Devon skittered to Travis' side. He turned him over onto his stomach and hissed out a breathe. "Oh fuck. That thing nearly peeled you."

"How bad is it?" Travis managed to ask while the mad creature continued its assault on the door.

"Not bad." Devon's voice quavered and he wouldn't meet Travis's eyes. After a moment he forced a smile and then stood and walked away.

"You're a terrible liar," Travis said to his retreating shape. "It's one of the reasons I love you." He gasped as he shifted to a sitting position. His shirt damp with blood sticking to skin and his bandages a tattered ruin now.

"I'm dying," he said, crumpling back onto his belly. "I don't want to die." The pain raked from his butt to his collarbone. "Gods, please help me."

"Quiet now," Devon said. Travis blinked at him. He hadn't heard his return. "Lay still so I can clean the cuts."

Travis did as he was told, groaning loudly as he bent and moved.

"Sorry hun, but this is going to hurt." Devon poured something that burned onto the wounds.

A shriek tried to crawl from Travis's mouth like a giant many-legged bug. Travis trapped it in his throat, cutting off his ability to breathe.

The ground swayed under him, and he drifted away.

AEON

Aeon heard the shriek. It was distant, but distinct, like Aeon was hearing it in his bones instead of with his ears.

The crowd stopped chattering like hungry rats and went silent. Their faces were masks of shock, panic, and despair. *Perfect.* Aeon could not have asked for a better moment.

"Did you hear that?" Rita asked. "We are not going to let you open that door."

Aeon slammed his fist into the side of her head, sending her tumbling into the wall. She hit the stone with a dull whack and crumpled to the floor, leaving a small trail of blood down the gray brick. "Shut the fuck up. Do you hear me? If you say one more word I will kill you."

Rita's vision went dazed and unfocused. Rita touched the spot where her skull had smacked the wall, and revealed her bloody fingers. Aeon was sure she was going to say something, but there must have been something in his eyes that told her he wasn't lying. Good. Her time was done.

She nodded.

Aeon smiled, letting his rage curve his lips and fill his eyes. He turned his back on her.

"I'm done listening to these people," he said to the crowd. "This stopped being a job the moment that door slammed shut, and I'm done letting traitors to our species make decisions for us. It ain't right. We haven't heard from the bitch in days. Jackson neither. The faggots have abandoned us. They are probably through the gate already. Laughing at how stupid we are. And that bitch Candace probably went with them." Aeon paused, absorbing the fear and indecision emanating throughout the silent room, then pointed behind him.

"I'm getting that door open. I'm heading to the control room. And I'm damned sure gonna make them all pay for leaving us here to look like fools. Anyone who wants to stop me can join them on the corpse pile."

Aeon pulled his work knife from its sheath and pointed it at the crowd, moving slowly in a circle before landing on Rita, who still huddled against the wall.

No one moved to stop him.

"Now bitch, you're gonna make this clip work," he purred.

TRAVIS

ang! Bang! Bang! Bang!

BTravis came to with a jolt. A fog of weariness enveloped him, his senses dull and sharp at the same time. His back seared, and his head throbbed. All he could see from where he lay on his stomach was the floor and the wall adjoining it. Behind him Devon tugged on his skin as he taped bandages to his wounds and the creature attacked the door. Travis flinched with every bang and steel-tearing screech that tore through the walls like tissue paper.

Devon rolled him over onto his back as gently as possible but the motion was still like being doused in lava. Travis bit his tongue to keep himself from crying out.

"I'm sorry," Travis said

Devon's eyebrows shot up. "Why?"

Slowly Travis pulled himself into a sitting position and used the wall to hold himself up. He wiped away the tears that marred his dusty cheeks. His throat was raw and he coughed dryly.

"For having the stupid idea that I could do something to help. For letting you tag along. For not listening to Candace.

Take your pick." Travis forced a grin and looked around to try to find something that might contain water or something to drink.

Devon shook his head and walked away, disappearing down one of the rows of lockers. A moment later he came back with an arm full of water bottles. He handed one to Travis.

"You always do this, you know," Devon said.

"Do what?" Travis unscrewed the bottle with trembling hands and took a long drink of the tepid water.

"Act like you don't need anyone. I get that you don't like being around everyone, but you can't do everything on your own. And this" — Devon gestured into the air — "isn't your fault. I am my own man. I make my own decisions."

"I never said you weren't your own man."

"Quiet. It's fine. *We* are fine. I love you. And you were right in there. More than ever, we need to get out of here. That thing out there will kill us all. I don't know what it is or why it's here, but I know that." Devon said. "And you're the only one here who knows how the gate works."

Travis frowned. He wondered how the thing had gotten out of the hangar and how he could get the survivors from the rec room to the gate with it prowling the halls. And what should he do about Candace?

"I appreciate your confidence in my abilities, but we are truly screwed right now," said Travis.

Boom, boom, boom.

The force of the monster slamming into the locker room door sounded like drum beats echoing around them. The stone wall around the door cracked. How strong was that thing? Could it really break through the wall?

"With that thing outside, we aren't going anywhere. Not to the control room and not back for the others." Travis finished the rest of his water, stood, and hobbled to the trash can and threw it in. The pain was still excruciating, but Travis could wrap his mind around it now and manage it.

Bam. Bam. BAM. BAM. BAM.

"Shut up, we get it!" Travis screamed at the door.

Devon slumped over on the bench. Deflated, pale, and shaking. Reality was not something that Travis wanted to deal with, but he thought it better than false optimism. Avoiding the issue rang too close to Candace's flawed logic.

"Come on," Travis said. "Let's move away from the door." He held out a hand to Devon and lifted him to his feet. The torn skin of his back pulled at the bandages. He groaned in pain.

"We should let the others know what is going on," Devon said.

Travis nodded. "Good idea." He pulled up the comms menu on his clip, found the intercom system, and selected the rec room.

"Hello," Travis said and waited for a response. "This is Travis and Devon. You all still there?"

He and Devon sat on a bench on the other side of the locker room as far from the door and the creature as they could get. Travis shivered. How long will that fancy space-aged metal hold?

RITA

Rita reached the transmitter first. Propelled by relief bordering on joy and true hope. Aeon was only a few steps behind her. As she pressed the mic button, he ripped the box out of her hand.

"What?" he barked.

Those in the room were silent. Rita stared at each of them in turn, seeing the same hope and anticipation written on their faces.

Travis's voice shook when he spoke. "I just wanted to let you all know what was going on. We made it to the locker room, but we are stuck here now."

A murmur of confusion and concern erupted behind Rita, but quieted when Aeon lifted his hand. Rita took a step away, wanting to melt back into the crowd.

"Why are you stuck? You got the maintenance suits. You got the air to breathe. What's the problem?" Aeon sounded calm, but she didn't believe he'd stay that way.

"We got attacked by something and barely made it here. The thing has us cornered, and we have no way out." There was a long pause before Travis continued. "I don't know how long we have before it breaks down the door."

"Right." Aeon laughed. "Right. Now there are scary monsters. Mmhmm. Well, we are working on getting ourselves out of here, and we will say hi to your monster on our way to the gate. Anything else you want to tell us? Want us to bring you a cookie?" With a flourish he dropped the transmitter. It swung on its wire and smacked into the wall with a plastic *thuck.*

"Please do NOT leave the room," Travis shouted. "You don't understand. Please. Do NOT leave that room . . . . Someone say something."

The mass of people parted as Aeon shoved his way through the crowd. As he passed them, they murmured questions and remarks Rita couldn't decipher. She hated that the crowd was his now. They'd done nothing when he'd hit her. Not one even asked if she was okay or needed help.

Were they not going to listen? Did they not understand? Travis wouldn't lie about something like this. If he said there was something out there, then there was. What that information changed about her situation she didn't know. She was still trapped here with a psycho while Travis and Devon were trapped in the locker room. *What options did she have?*

"Hey," someone said. Rita turned to find a short blond-haired man from the new crew standing close to her.

He looked around to make sure that no one was listening and said, "Can you help me?"

"I don't know? Depends."

The man licked his lips. "Look, Aeon is fucking nuts. And if he manages to get that door open and doesn't kill himself and all of us doing it, I'd like to have the gate working so we can get the fuck out of here before he can fuck it up."

Rita narrowed her eyes and wondered what this man was getting at. The bruise on her face and the welt on the back of her skull ached a reminder to her. "So? What can I do about any of that? I'm trapped here, and Travis is trapped there. So, what do you want me to do?"

A smile spread across the man's face. "You? You don't have to do much. Just get plugged into that box, and I think I can get those guys to the gate. Beyond that I, well . . . beyond that, we will just have to hope that this Travis guy can do something."

Rita peered around the man. Most of the others were watching Aeon work: cheering him on, offering suggestions, talking loudly about how they'd all been betrayed. The ones who weren't were huddled together, talking quietly. The room was a tinderbox lusting for a spark to ignite.

Across the room, Aeon and his cronies were examining the open instrument panel. A red-headed woman pulled at the wires dangling out of the door's control panel trying to figure out how to attach the wires to his clip, but it wasn't going well. How long before he decided to test the connection with someone else? Rita was afraid she would be his first experiment.

"Fine," she said, turning around and exposing her clip. "Take the little thing out, but be quick about it. I don't want anyone to see."

The man nodded. There was a slight tug on her neck as he removed the camera and another as he pulled out the little piece beneath it. He slipped it into her hand without saying a word and then walked away.

Rita studied the details of the small device. It was smaller than her finger nail. A bit of plastic covered circuitry with a thin sliver of metal protruding from the bottom. *Was this the right idea?* If someone saw, if someone said something to Aeon, Aeon would probably kill her. That guy was crazy and, from what she could see, most of the others were willing to follow him. It was just more convenient to believe everyone else was lying than to accept the danger they faced.

She took a step toward the forgotten transmitter and then moved farther along the far wall towards the middle of the room. All she had to do was plug the little piece into the bottom of the box, and then she could walk away to talk to Travis. She thanked God the transmitter was near the useless pool tables. No one else was near them.

Her heart pounded with each step. There were too many eyes, too many conversations that stalled when she walked past, too much tension pouring off of them all. Every flicker of movement brought bile up her throat. *Be careful,* she told herself, *move slowly but naturally.*

There were more people standing around the transmitter that still dangled from the wall by its cord. They were talking quietly to each other, asking when they thought this would all be done or why Candace and Travis would lie to them. A few were even angrily muttering about the rightness of it all. The unfairness.

Her hand found the cord attached to the box. With her back to it and the wall, she began to slide the wire through her fingers, inch by inch, waiting for any sign that someone had noticed what she was doing. The only one watching her, though, was the blond man who approached her.

Finally, the box was in her hand. It almost slipped from her sweaty fingers as she gently touched it, using her finger tips to feel for the correct port to plug her clip into.

"I can't wait to see the look on that guy's face when we show up at the gate," someone near her said.

"Yeah," said another voice. "Gonna be a big fucking surprise for all three of them. Probably watching and laughing at us right now."

"Can you believe that monster bullshit? I mean. Come on. That bitch probably fucked something up, and now that guy and his boyfriend are helping her cover it up."

Rita touched the hole next to the piece of Travis's clip that was still lodged in place. She pressed the piece into the box. There was a faint pop in her ears. *That's done.*

Sparks popped and sizzled from the back of Aeon's clip on the other side of the room and the sound of laughter that followed drowned out the noise the transmitter made tapping listlessly on the stone as she let the cord slide through her fingers.

"Fuck," Aeon shouted and shoved the redhead into the wall. She smacked the stone hard and left a trail of blood on the gray brick as she collapsed in a heap on the floor.

"Hard part is over," Rita mumbled to herself and walked slowly back to the blond man.

TRAVIS

"Travis? Travis, this is Rita. Can you hear me?"

Travis nearly dropped his bottle of water. Devon stopped his pacing and spun around to face Travis.

"Yes, Rita, I can hear you. What is going on?"

Rita sighed. "Thank God this worked. Are you still doing alright?"

"Yeah. I don't know how much longer we will be, though. That thing is gonna bash down the wall soon."

Devon came and sat next to Travis. He smelled of sweat, and it mingled with the stale smell of urine emanating from a puddle in the corner of the room. Travis needed to take a dump, but he wasn't ready to do that in the corner just yet. Time would probably change his mind, but only if they lived that long.

"Fantastic," Rita said. Her voice was faint, but he could hear the sarcasm in her whisper. "I got a guy here from the new crew who thinks he can help you and Devon get to the gate."

Relief flooded through Travis, but he killed it. He needed to keep his head on straight, and pessimism was better for that. If he started to hope, or believe, it would make it easier for him to make a mistake.

"That's great," he said tentatively. "What is his plan?"

The comms went silent for a moment. Travis guessed she was discussing it with this new person. Time stretched on, and fear crept back in. Had Aeon decided to stop her from talking? Had they opened the door and discovered that the halls had been repressurized?

Travis glanced at Devon, who was ready to vibrate off the bench, and then looked away. The thing outside thrashed and slammed into the wall. Dust sifted down from the ceiling and another fissure split the wall around the door. Travis shivered.

Travis's clip popped and crackled in his ear. "Travis?"

"Yeah Rita, I'm here. What's going on?

"Sorry. Things here are getting insane. Aeon is trying to build a bomb to blow up the door since he can't get that clip trick you did to work. People are freaking out. It's nuts." The words tumbled out in a high pitched rush. "No one believes you. They're too scared or too stupid to listen."

Another crack formed in the wall by the door.

"Rita? What is the plan? I don't think we have a lot of time here."

"Oh fuck, shit, yeah. So the guy works for maintenance and said that there should be a door leading to the maintenance tunnels in the locker room. You can use them to get to the gate then get back to us. So we should be able to get past the monster in the halls and out of the outpost."

Could it really be that easy? How had he not thought of this? He knew the tunnels existed and what they were for, but had never considered using them.

"What did she say?" Devon asked.

"She said we can use the maintenance tunnels to get to the gate."

Devon punched the air and clapped. "Whoo! Fantastic. Oh, this is amazing." Fresh tears welled in his eyes and streamed down his face, cutting little tracks in the smears of blood he hadn't washed off.

Travis couldn't help but smile too. "This is amazing news, Rita. How do we get to this door?"

There was a short silence before she answered, "He said that there should be a panel in the far right or left corner that can be opened with the clip. He said if you can't access it, use his access code of AlphaRed1."

Travis laughed as tears of relief fought their way out. "Thank you," he said. "Now you be careful, got it? We will let you know when we reach the gate."

"We'll try," she said. "You two be safe too."

Travis stood and walked over to the far-left corner of the room. The skin on his back wailed in protest as each step pulled open the wounds. The panel they needed was easy to find. It was in the direct line of sight of the quickly-fracturing wall. The door was beginning to push inward. Soon he would be able to glimpse the hall on the other side. "I think this is going to work out," Devon said, his face bright with excitement.

Bang. Bang. Claws scrabbling over stone and metal digging trenches into every surface. It screeched in frustration.

Travis disagreed, but kept this to himself. The monster outside was narrowing their chance of escape with every strike against the wall.

"Get two of the suits," he said.

As Devon wandered off, Travis examined the door to the maintenance tunnels. It sat flush with the gray wall, but the seam was evident once he knew what to look for. Opening it was easy, and he was thankful he didn't need the access code. If they needed to run, having to use the code would cost them precious time. Time they likely wouldn't have. Unlike other doors, this one opened inward. At first he thought it was flimsy but it was thick and was fitted with pins like a vault door.

Devon returned with two of the flimsy blue plastic suits in one hand and two of the backpacks that held the air supply in the other. He joined Travis in silently staring into the utter blackness of the maintenance tunnel.

There were supposed to be overhead fluorescents. Travis wondered if this was due to the explosion or if they had to manually be turned on. If the latter was true, Travis could not find any command to do so.

"Well, shit my britches," Devon said. "I'm not going in there, suit or no suit. Fuck that. Nope."

The creature flailed wildly against the wall with increased vigor.

"I don't see how we have a choice," Travis said flatly.

The black seemed to mock him. *Come on. Nothing bad ever happened in the dark.* A shiver ran down his spine, his cuts burning as his muscles twitched. The pain was a fresh reminder that the danger was behind the locked door and not the open one.

"Get your suit on," Travis said. "We can leave the hoods off for now, and I can light our way with my clip camera. And the infrared feature will tell us if there are any more of those things down there." The remaining color on Devon's face vanished, leaving Travis wishing he hadn't shattered his boyfriend's naive excitement. Apparently, they had different ideas of what might be in the dark.

"Oh-oh-oh okay," Devon stammered.

Travis forced a smile. "We got nothing to worry about down there," he said. "This door has a triple seal on it. That should keep the monster out — if it makes it through the door that is. Once we are in the tunnels, I want you to head back to the rec room and wait for me. I'll let Rita know if and when I get the gate working. If I can't, we can at least make a plan for outlasting this nightmare."

"You're gonna leave me? Alone? Down there?"

Travis wanted to strangle his partner. Didn't Devon understand that he was helping him get back to safety? "Look —"

"No, *you* look. I am fucking tired of you trying to ditch me. I know I am not as smart as you, and I probably have a life of this to look forward to at home, but if that's what it is, just say it.

Stop being a coward and using convenience to do your work for you."

Travis's temper flared. His mind emptied of everything except for anger and pity. "You really are stupid. But I love you. I don't love you for it, or in spite of it. I just love you. And honestly, my life would be a lot easier if I didn't. But it wouldn't be better."

Travis took a deep breath and clenched his fists tighter. "I'm sending you back because there is literally nothing you can do to help me. Nothing. Literally nothing. There is only more potential danger if you come with me. It's safer if you go back. You can help me if you go back, calm down everyone in the rec room and help them get to safety when the time is right. Get it. You can either walk into danger for no reason or toward safety for a good reason."

They glared at each other. "Do you get it now?" Travis growled. "I'm being pragmatic, but I'm also watching out for you and the only one watching out for everyone still alive on this flipping rock. Someone needs to make sure everyone has a chance to escape. But Candace is trying to starve us to death and that fuck Aeon is convincing everyone to commit suicide. It feels like it's fucking pointless. Is it? Am I crazy for trying to protect people?"

"Am I allowed to speak now, sir," Devon asked after a moment.

Travis rolled his eyes and waved his hand to say 'go ahead.'

"You know, everyone told me what an asshole you were, but I never saw it 'til now. But I'll listen to your wise judgment, sir. You know best." Devon stalked away and began to put on his own suit.

The anger that had overtaken Travis quickly fled. He wanted to rush over and apologize to Devon, but thought better of it. Devon's safety was more important than their relationship. And if that was the cost to ensure Devon lived through this, he would gladly pay it.

They dressed in silence. The only noise was the soft crinkle of the plastic suits and the occasional steel screams of the creature in its continued siege on the door. The two men lifted the tanks of air onto each other's backs and attached the hoses to the ports in the back of the suits.

Travis's back seethed under the weight.

They picked up their helmets, and Travis led the way into the darkness. Once through the door, he ordered it to close and plunged them into total blackness. The sound of their breathing was more unsettling than the lack of light. A stale, wet, musty scent filled their nostrils. The smell was powerfully reminiscent of the pond behind his grandmother's home on Earth. He wondered if he would soon see cattails down here or hear the croak of frogs.

"I'm sorry," Travis muttered as he pulled the camera out of the clip and ordered it to turn on. It began to hover, and the brilliant LED light ignited, revealing their way. The little drone's camera feed popped into his field of vision. Travis instructed it to fly forward a few feet.

"I know you are," Devon grumbled. "For what it's worth, I am too."

Travis grabbed Devon's hand and squeezed. It wasn't the same with the suit on, but he tried to put everything unsaid into the gesture. After a moment of hesitation, Devon squeezed back.

"Should, uh, should we, you know, get going?" Devon asked.

"Yeah," Travis said, turning to face Devon. "But first . . ." He leaned in and kissed Devon. It was gentle at first, but it quickly became more. Travis tasted hot tears on his partner's lips when he pulled away.

"I love you," Travis whispered. They touched their foreheads and embraced each other. Stupid as it was, Travis feared this would be the last time he saw Devon, and suddenly he wanted to change his mind and tell Devon to come with him.

"I love you too. And you are right. This is better."

With that, Devon pulled away, stepping deeper into the tunnel.

Travis caught up to him, and the two moved quietly together, guided by the light of the drone until they came to a steep drop off and a ladder leading down. How deep the ladder went was impossible to guess, but he supposed they were about to find out.

"I'll go first," Travis said. "See you at the bottom."

CANDACE

"What the hell? What the fucking fuck? God dammit!" Candace howled. She watched in horror as the remaining survivors did one stupid thing after another. It didn't bother her that the idiot Aeon had gathered all of the booze in the rec room to try and burn his way out. In her mind, the fifty-three people in there were already dead. Thinking of them like that made everything easier, but Travis and Devon were continuing to piss her off.

What could she do about it though? In the last hour she had been pouring over the control panel, trying to decipher the rest of what it could do while the larger creature and its fleshy, multi-faced, multi-limbed form stalked the hangar. *Why had she never bothered to learn how to use these fucking things?*

She needed the controls that would allow her to open and close any door in the outpost. The gate was nearly whole, and if Travis was able to get it working . . .

The thought of venting out the air had come to her when Travis and Devon were in the locker room, but they had put those fucking suits on, rendering the idea useless. Why hadn't they just come here like they had said they would? The monster would have gotten to them first, but if it hadn't, then they would have seen what was in the hangar and understood *why* they couldn't leave.

Why wouldn't anyone listen to her? Maybe she should risk a walk to the armory and grab a rifle. Almost no one knew they had guns here, not even Travis, but it was a risk she couldn't take. If that monster in the halls killed her, then there would be no one to stop Travis, and that left billions of people on Drexel 7 at risk, and the billions more connected to the planet through its other gates. No, the answer was the door controls.

"They should have left the fucking manuals here. This is so fucking stupid."

"Yeah, well, maybe I could have helped you," Candace said in a high falsetto, imitating Jackson whose carcass smelled so bad she couldn't help but vomit every time she breathed heavily.

"Well," she said in response. "If you hadn't been an asshole and put all those lives at risk, I wouldn't have had to kill you."

She laughed. It roiled out of her like a clown and she couldn't stop herself. She laughed until she couldn't breathe, and when she sucked in air, her laughter turned to retching. Bile and spit coated her mouth until her abs throbbed from the spasming.

"Laugh all you want. If you hadn't been so quick to murder, you might have considered working with me and Travis. We might have even found a solution that saved everyone *and* prevented the creature from escaping. You might even have gotten to see Julia again."

Saying the words were a salve for her guilt, even if she had to pretend it was Jackson saying them in order to get them out.

"Too late for that now," she said. "Way too late." Her stomach growled. The hunger cramps had finally grabbed her.

"It really isn't," the falsetto voice intoned. "You could still try to do the right thing. Travis thinks he understands, but he doesn't. You could try and flush that monster out of the hangar and let Travis have his try."

"No!" she yelled. "It's done! Enough. *Gods*. Enough. Enough blood is on my hands already. I won't have any more."

Candace studied the monitor as her own words reverberated around her. Fifty-three more bodies in the rec room and two in the tunnels beneath the outpost. Then the murdering would be done. She stole a glance at the Avealus Gate. It was nearly repaired, but thankfully that would not be enough for the thing to escape. As long as no one reset the power, the gate would never turn on and the monster would be trapped here.

Candace whimpered as a spike of pain lanced behind her eyes.

"Keep it up, fucker, but I got you." She chuckled. Something warm trickled down her face and ran down her cheek. When she wiped it away, her hand came back covered in a thin layer of blood.

She rubbed at her eyes and she saw movement on the monitor — the feed from the camera inside the locker room. The thing had finally made it through the door. The monster scattered debris everywhere as it tore through the room. It yanked out lockers from the floor and launched them into each other.

The destruction was beautiful.

Candace had damned herself, made an endless stream of mistakes since she had noticed the first vibrations. Every death since, and every death to come, was on her, but she wouldn't let herself make another mistake. She had to make the hard choices, *the right choices*. She had to put the lives of billions of strangers before those of her friends and colleagues despite whatever that meant for her soul. *It was the only way.*

Nothing could kill these monsters, and she wouldn't let it leave here. She would find a way to kill Travis, and that would be the end of it. She only wished she could have talked to Julia one last time. It would have been enough just to see her wife's beautiful face and hear her laugh before she died, but it wasn't meant to be.

DEVON

Devon heard a distant boom from above. The monster was in the locker room now. Bangs and screams denoted its rampage of the area they had just been. He swiveled to Travis.

"Go," Travis said firmly.

Devon gazed into the dark tunnel in front of him. He couldn't do this. Not alone. "I can't," he moaned.

"Yes, you can," Travis answered. "Just follow this tunnel. Go quickly, and go quietly. Once you get to the end, Rita says there will be a ladder that leads up to the rec room. Once you get there, you'll figure out what to do next. If the monster gets down here, have everyone take the halls upstairs. If it's up there then bring them down here. Real easy."

Devon chuckled nervously. None of that sounded easy. It sounded terrifying, but he would do it. He had to. *For Travis.*

"Okay," Devon said. He licked his lips and flexed his shaking hands. The sounds from above grew louder. Whatever was after them had moved on to busting its way through the door to the tunnel. How long the door would last, he couldn't guess, but he hoped it lasted longer than the other. The images of that thing throwing him to the ground and tearing him open invaded his mind.

"Go," Travis said. "I love you. Go."

Devon didn't trust himself to speak, so he turned, only looking back once to see Travis disappear behind a pillar.

The darkness swallowed Devon as he walked slowly down the tunnel. He kept his hand against the wall as he walked, bumping into air tanks, canisters of cleaning solution, and random crates of supplies every few feet. Each time he hit something, he stumbled and lost contact with the wall.

Each time, panic flickered to life, certain he wouldn't be able to find the wall again and would be lost in the emptiness until the monster found him. Soon his fingers would touch the wall and he would breathe easy. It went like this until he was certain he was in the wrong tunnel and would never find his way to the ladder. Then he walked face first into a wall and tumbled to the ground. He shouted out in pain and joy. He was there. He'd made it. Safety was only a few short feet and a quick climb away.

Boom!

The sound echoed through the tunnel and rattled his bones. The metal door separating him and Travis from the monster clanked to the ground behind him.

The savage monster was here with them.

Devon jumped to his feet and patted at the wall looking for the metal rungs of the ladder.

Bang!

The sound was deafening. Devon had thought he was farther away from where they had started, but he was wrong. So very wrong.

He patted the wall harder and faster, taking no care to be quiet. *Where is it? Where is the fucking ladder?* Why hadn't he listened to Travis. It was stupid of him to come. He was going to die down here. He was going to die in the dark, alone and scared.

Metal. His hand struck metal. He patted it again and welcomed the familiar round shapes of the rungs pressed against his palm. Without a pause he frantically began his climb. He was going to make it. Only fifteen or twenty feet to go. No problem. Hand, foot, hand, foot. He climbed as fast as he could.

He was going to live. No thoughts or worries about Travis existed in his mind at that moment. At that moment he only had space in him for the metal ladder and the hatch above.

In the distance the monster screamed. Closer now.

TRAVIS

oom!

The echo was much louder this time. Travis had taken for granted the thickness of the door and the solidness of the locks until he heard the metal door slamming against the ladder the whole way down into the tunnel. He stopped and turned back.

Bang!

Travis covered his ears to block out the noise that reverberated off the narrow walls. The monster was inside the tunnel and it had brought the buzzing down here with it, so loud now that it was perceptible with all of his senses. It both felt and tasted like licking a battery.

Silence.

It must have stopped moving. Would the thing follow him or go after Devon? Devon didn't have a light, or a camera, so there should be no way for the monster to know which way he had gone, but that was true for him as well. Had they gotten far enough away that the monster wouldn't be able to find them?

The click of claws echoed, but Travis couldn't tell which direction it headed.

"Shifty sticks," he mumbled to himself. If Rita's directions were accurate, the ladder he needed wasn't far away, but nothing down here resembled what she described. He would just have to trust her and hope he would find the ladder long before the thing found him. What about Devon? *You messed up. He should have come along with you. If something happens to him, it'll be your fault.* The thought made what little control he still had over his full bladder fail, and a small trickle of urine escaped. He needed to help him somehow.

"Devon!" he shouted into the black tunnels. "Run!"

A metallic screech pierced his ears, making the air thick and his brain numb. *Good,* he thought. *Come get me.*

Travis turned back and ordered the camera light off and its infrared function on. He had no idea if this would work. The thing was invisible, but he hoped it gave off heat.

Quickly he began to move. Not in the direction he thought he needed to go, but off to the left. Travis needed to distract the thing. Keep it busy so it wouldn't go after Devon. And if the camera actually worked and he stayed quiet enough, he might still be able to make it out alive.

"Hey! Devon. If you can hear me, it's down here." The words bounced down the tunnels and rebounded back to him. He didn't wait for the reply. Instead, he ran three junctions down and hid around a corner. His camera drone followed after him, watching his back.

Travis remembered from before he'd turned off the light that the hall stretched down to his right, broken up at different points with junctions or ladders leading up. Somewhere down one of these tunnels was a ladder that led to the waiting area off of the hangar.

Something flashed on the camera. Travis returned his attention to the feed. He expected a normal thermal image or just heat residue from where the thing's feet touched the floor, but that was not what he saw.

What he saw was the absence of an image in the shape of the monster — the walls, floor, even the air gave off small traces of heat, creating an imprint of its form. It was moving negative space, six legged, and seven feet high, and nearly filling the entire tunnel. The monster swayed as it walked, swiveling its head from side to side. It turned right and disappeared from view.

Travis crept backward, careful of the placement of his feet so as to not create any noise this time. Not when that fucker was this close. He left the camera where it was, though. The creature didn't seem to notice it, and Travis would continue to let it spy for him.

At the next junction, he paused. Left, right, or straight? Left was out as an option as that would bring him closer to the monster. He needed to go right eventually, but that would leave him exposed 'til he got to the next turn.

The creature moved along slowly in parallel with Travis. As cautiously as Travis. The camera followed, but kept its distance. Its head swayed back and forth rhythmically. Details of its features were still not distinguishable, but Travis had a vivid enough imagination. In his mind the monster was a scaly six-legged cat the size of a small elephant.

Pick a lane. There were only a few seconds until the thing would be at the same junction, and then what? Straight. He stepped out into the open, the plastic of his suit under his feet crinkling with each step. *Crinkle. crinkle. Crinkle. crinkle.*

His mouth ran dry. The camera captured the stalking blank space as it neared the junction he'd just crossed. Travis struggled to keep the slower pace across the next intersection. Rivers of sweat soaked his clothes, and he desperately needed to pee.

Once he was hidden from view by the wall, he pulled the maintenance suit over his head. Slowly. Millimeter by millimeter. Every crinkle of the plastic a potential give away. It clicked into place and hissed as it sealed. Fresh air flooded in, and Travis fought the urge to take a deep breath. He hoped that the suit masked his smell from the monster.

The monster stopped. He watched in the camera feed as it

jerked its head toward where he stood. The camera drifted forward a bit before he ordered it to stop. The sudden braking made the little servos hum. The monster's head whipped around to stare right at the floating white disc. It took a step toward it.

Something crashed off in the distance. *Tink, tink, tink, tink, tink, tink.*

Devon. It had to be.

"Fuck." Travis blinked. The monster was gone. The camera bobbed up and down in the wake of the wind created by the monster's sudden running. The sound of its clicking claws quickly faded, heading right for Devon.

The monster screeched. Why did it sound joyous?

Travis chased after it, his heart thrashed in his chest. Images of what that thing would do to Devon — *God, Devon*. Not Devon. Not like this. They had so much left to do together. So much life left to live. Vacations to take, arguments to have. They still needed to meet each other's parents, grow old together, grow tired of each other. He wasn't sure what to do when he caught up with it. *If* he could catch up with it. But he needed to do something. *Anything.* Devon would not die here today, in the dark, alone.

DEVON

"Devon! Run!" Travis's voice was faint, nearly drowned out by the screech that had followed, but Devon did as he was ordered. He flew up the ladder faster, only slipping and nearly falling once before he reached the top. His head collided with the metal door. Pain flared and coursed across his lightly-battered skull. His hands slipped on the rung and his back struck the side of the tube. He wobbled in the cramped space, using the walls of the tunnel to keep from falling all the way down.

"Hey! Devon. If you can hear me, it's down here."

I know! Now shut up or it will get you too.

"Hello?" said a voice from above him.

He jolted, almost falling again.

"Yes?" he whispered. "This is Devon, can you hear me?"

There was a long moment of silence and then, "Yes. What is going on?" It was Rita. Her voice was muffled by the hatch door, but it was clearly her.

"Let me up. Let me up now," Devon stammered. He pushed against the door again. How was he supposed to open it? Was there a trick he didn't know?

"I don't know how."

"Get the maintenance guy to do it."

"Okay. Stay calm."

Stay calm? Stay fucking calm? Devon climbed until he could use his shoulder to push against the hatch, but he might as well have been pushing a mountain for all the good it did.

"Devon?" Rita asked. "Devon, you need to get Travis. Corin said you need to use the clip to open it. The hatches are just like any other door."

"What?" Devon said in a hysterical screech. "I can't. It's down here. The thing is down here. Open the door. Pry it open if you have to. *Just do it now.* Do it!"

"We'll try," Rita said. "Aeon give us your knife. Now! We're gonna pry up the hatch."

Shouting and commotion erupted above. What was going on? What was he going to do? If they couldn't get the hatch open, he couldn't stay here, but where could he go? That thing was below him, and there was nowhere he could hide. What could he do?

"Devon?" a male voice he didn't recognize said. "Listen. We are gonna try and pry the hatch from our end, but I don't know if it will work. The pins on these hatches are weak. Is there something down there you can use to try and break it?"

Devon didn't know. His mind was blank.

"Were there any spare air canisters?" the voice asked. "Maybe you can use it as a battering ram?"

"Okay," Devon said, but he didn't move.

Getting what he needed would mean going back down into the tunnels, back to where the monster was. His body floated, disconnected from his mind. *Move. Move for fucks sake.* He took a step down, then another, each step harder than the one before it. Then he was at the bottom.

When his feet came in contact with the floor, he froze. The buzzing came flooding back into his brain as if the monster was right on top of him. How he knew that, he couldn't have said, but he knew. It took all of his remaining will power to pry his fingers off the rung and move out into the tunnel. He dragged his fingers along the wall next to the ladder until he found where the wall joined another.

Methodically he pressed on, keeping one hand on the wall, the other probing the air for obstacles and obstructions. After a few feet, Devon found what he was searching for: A group of empty air canisters bundled together with a cord and pushed up against the wall. As he pulled on one, it scraped along the other canisters.

"Crap." The bundle of air tanks clanked and wobbled. He inched the air tank out from the bundle. The cord wrapped around them snapped like a rubber band. An explosion of metal against metal resounded through the tunnel as the other canisters banged into each other and fell in a pile to the floor, rolling in opposite directions.

The monster screamed. The sound rolled ahead of it down the long dark tunnel.

Devon sprinted, tripped on a canister, and sprawled to the ground. He scrambled to his feet, grabbing the canister as he got up, and ran back to the ladder, climbing as fast as he could. The monster would be coming for sure. There was no way it hadn't heard all of that. He needed to climb.

"Open the hatch," he squawked through a dry throat.

No one answered.

He banged a fist on the door.

"It's coming," Devon shouted. "Open it."

"We're trying," Rita answered.

"Open the fucking hatch," Devon shouted as he slammed the air canister against the hatch. It wouldn't budge.

"We're trying," Rita shouted back. "We don't know how!"

Fuck. I'm going to die.

The monster screamed. It was almost right below him.

"What was that?" someone above him asked.

"Help me! Please!" Devon shrieked as he hammered against the hatch door.

"Get it open!" Rita shouted.

"Hell no," someone else said. "We aren't letting that thing in here."

"Open it! Please. Don't leave me down here!" Devon cried. "Please!"

He cocked his arm to bash the canister into the door. His foot slipped on the rung. His hand shot out to grab onto the ladder. He missed. His back struck the wall and bounced him forward. His head smacked the metal rung. A pain of many colors filled his vision. Dazed, he fell. His hands and feet made a strumming noise as they skittered over the metal. A few feet from the bottom, Devon was finally able to grab a rung. His arm jolted. His grip slipped off the rung and tumbled, slamming hard into the floor below.

Devon groaned and spat blood. He'd bitten his tongue, and he was sure he'd broken his arm and his legs. Pain like a thousand knives lanced every inch of his body enveloping him in a cocoon of lightning, sharp and distinct. It was a miracle he hadn't died. Black that had nothing to do with the darkness of the tunnel crept in along the edges of his vision.

The sound of long fingernails drumming on a table drifted towards him.

"Travis," Devon moaned. "Travis?"

The monster growled and sniffed. It seemed only inches away.

"Travis," Devon squealed. He couldn't hear his own voice over the buzzing that invaded his mind. "Travis! Help me!"

TRAVIS

"Travis! Help me!"

That scream. Oh God, that scream.

"Devon!"

"Travis!"

Devon continued wailing. Travis could feel Devon's desperation. It tore at his heart. Travis bolted down the tunnel following closely behind. Closer. Closer. Then, after one terrible tearing sound, the screaming stopped. It sounded like — like . . . like skin being torn off, then the sound of gushing water. *Blood. It had to be blood.* He could see it clearly in his mind, vivid and red. He was so close, maybe only feet away.

His legs burned with the strain of his sprinting. Travis stopped himself by running into a wall to cease his momentum. Slamming into it with a thud. The cuts on his back seared with fresh agony, and he could feel the bandages soaking up fresh blood.

It can't be. Please scream again. Travis sobbed. *Even that sound is better than silence.*

Another wet tearing sound. Then a thud as something flopped onto the floor. *Wet. Wetwetwetwet. Devon. Please, not Devon. No. It should have been me.*

His whole body shook with the effort to keep from bawling. *Go back. There is nothing you can do. Nothing. Nothing. Finish what you've started. Grieve later.*

But how?

The tearing sounds stopped. Silence stretched, broken only by the sound of Travis's panting breath. A tentative step. The click of claws.

Go.

The first step backward was almost impossible, but the second was easier, and each one after that easier still.

Travis glanced at the camera feed as he turned and saw the cooling remains of the man he loved in the tunnel behind him.

I am so sorry, Devon. I love you.

The noise of the suit as he stepped was excruciatingly loud. He considered taking the time to remove it, but it wasn't truly an option. That fucker would be on him quickly if he stopped moving, and taking the suit off would be noisier than just walking would be.

Travis moved farther away from Devon and the creature. The time for weaving and hiding had passed. Now he needed to find the ladder to the gate.

Behind him the camera slowly hovered. No image of the creature. After a minute, Travis wondered if maybe it had continued on in the other direction. Then something flashed across the camera's feed. He couldn't see what it was, but there was only one other thing down there with him, and it was moving. The camera spun around and attempted to follow the shape that had flashed past. But all Travis saw in the feed was an empty tunnel. Had it made a turn? Was it hiding now? Travis slowed his pace. He hugged the wall as he moved and listened. The clicking of claws resounded all around him.

Travis crept on, but every tunnel looked the same and he had no idea if he was even going in the right direction. While he walked, he kept an eye on the camera feed for any sign of the monster and an ear open for the sound of its claws clicking on stone.

He came back to the ladder that led up to the locker room. *How had he gotten this far off track?*

"Travis!" the voice of Devon called.

The blood in Travis's body turned to ice, and he froze with it.

"Travis!" The word came to him from far away, carried elegantly in the silence of the tunnels.

A scream of reply lodged in his throat, locked behind his frozen tongue. Devon was dead. Sounds of his body being torn to bits mixed with screams that faded into distant echoes. Like a ball bouncing away down the stone corridor until it became a roll that vanished into nothing. His camera caught it all: Flashes of movement as it tore and the vibrant reds and yellows of heat turning to blues and greens as Devon's corpse cooled on the tunnel floor.

Travis's grip on reality slipped. This wasn't real. *Move.* Devon was de — gone. No! It was a prank. A joke. Ha ha. *Move dang it. Don't die down here like —* The thought gave him the will to keep going and he began to trot as fast as he could without actually running. *Find the ladder. Climb the ladder.* And he would. Now that he was back at the start it was easy to find the quickest path to his destination and he moved along it. Noise be damned.

Sweat poured out of him. His chest burned, and his back ached. Every few turns he made, he thought he saw the monster in his camera feed, like *actually* saw it. It was just a hazy blob of heat, but only in fleeting moments.

Ignore it. Find the ladder. Climb the ladder.

He turned right down the final tunnel — the one he needed — and stopped. Cautiously he stepped towards the ending of this nightmare until something solid and heavy connected with his boot and heard the sound crunching under his heel. He bent to see what it was. His fingers probed gently in the utter darkness touching the object lightly. A flashlight, surrounded by a scatter of broken glass at the bottom of a ladder. Close to where he thought he needed to be, but why was it *here*? Was there someone else down here with him? Was that who he was seeing on the periphery of his vision?

Did it matter?

No.

"Help me Travis!" The voice was so close Travis imagined he could feel the monster's breath on the back of his neck.

Fudge it. Even if it wasn't the right ladder, it was close enough. He could find the gate easily enough once he was up above.

A large shape crept into view of the camera. It was the monster, but it was no longer a black hole that ate the heat around it, at least not entirely. The front half of it now gave off heat like any other creature while the back half was still missing from the image. It was hideous. Grotesque. Its body was covered in thin, swaying tendrils branching off in every direction, and its limbs more closely resembled the legs of a spider than a cat's. How could something so brittle-looking be so powerful?

Focus. The monster did not seem to know where he was, so there was still a chance for survival. Travis jittered forward, accidentally kicking the flashlight and sending it cascading down the tunnel.

Its head jerked towards the camera and Travis, who was not far away from it. "Travis!" Devon's voice called.

Travis gasped and ordered the camera drone's light on. He blinked in the sudden illumination. But Devon wasn't there. No, Devon was dead, and Travis just gave away his location.

"Mother biscuits." Travis gripped the rung of the ladder and began to climb up the side of the tunnel. Hand, foot, hand, foot. He was five feet in the air when the thing turned the corner into the same tunnel as Travis. The click of its claws made him turn back and the sight of it broke him. It wore Devon's face. His skin. His lover's body had been turned into a spindly, grotesque mockery of what he had been. Arms and legs too thin, too long, walking on all fours.

Travis screamed.

"Help me!" the monster cried. "Travis! It hurts!"

Climb. And he did. He raced up the ladder, his feet clanking the metal rungs in his panic.

The thing bolted down the tunnel. Travis was ten feet up when it reached the bottom of the ladder. The monster's face — Devon's face — stared up at Travis. The same face except for the eyes. The eyes were empty black holes.

"Come back. I love you," it told him.

Travis pushed himself to climb faster. Faster. At fifteen feet, he left the tunnel below and entered a tiny black column wide enough for a person and not much more. The thing followed, pulling itself up the ladder.

Travis gasped as his hand slipped and he fell, his fingers frantically seeking out the metal rungs, hunting for safety the way the monster hunted for him. After falling a few feet, his fingers gained purchase and his grip tightened around a rung. The jolting stop tore at his shoulder and agony ripped down the side of his body.

He howled in agony. The monster laughed.

There was no time to wallow in the pain. He climbed. Higher. The bolts holding the ladder to the wall groaned under the weight of the monster and the ladder began to pull away from the wall. Travis continued climbing until his head brushed a metal door. Travis pushed it, but it wouldn't budge. Below him, the massive monster had slowed its ascent, unable to squeeze its fleshy form into the small space blocking out the last of the light from his drone.

"Goddamn it," Travis shouted. "No. Open! Open!"

"Travis," the monster spoke quietly. The word drifted up to him like vapor. Travis peered down, seeing nothing but black, but he knew by the denseness of the blackness that the monster was close. He turned back to the door. There had to be a way to open it. He pulled up the door controls on his clip and frantically searched for the one that would open this hatch. The thing creeped up the ladder, inch by inch. Foot by foot. The click of its claws on metal and increasing buzz in his skull marked its increasing proximity.

Then, Travis found it: A tab marked Maintenance Controls. He opened the tab and clicked on the program that controlled the hatch system. A light on the door blinked yellow. An icon popped up on his clip asking if he wanted to open the hatch.

"Please. It hurts, Travis. It hurts so much," it whispered.

Travis blinked to confirm his escape. A mechanism in the hatch whirred, and the metal door popped open. Brilliant light flooded in, burning Travis's eyes as he scrambled up.

Something wet wrapped around his foot like a vine and yanked. Travis fell forward, his stomach rammed into the lip of the floor, knocking his breath out of him. The monster's arm yanked again. Travis braced his other foot on the top rung and pushed. The arm slipped on the plastic suit he wore. Travis dragged himself up and out of the hole. He kicked the arm. It slid further down his leg. He kicked again and tumbled across the floor, stopping just out its reach.

Devon's voice wailed in frustration. Travis spun back towards the hatch, and gazed into the tunnel. The light illuminated the grotesque beast that had tried to kill him. The putrid fudging butt licker screamed at him in his lover's voice, wearing his lover's face like a mask, his lover's skin stretched over bone and muscle like sheets thrown over furniture in a house closing up for the season.

The monster's arm stretched elastically, reaching towards Travis with Devon's fingers. Its claws grabbed at Travis as he forced the hatch down. It smashed the monster's outstretched hand. The monster yelped and thrashed and pushed its body against the door, forcing it back open. Travis threw himself onto the hatch slamming it back down onto the monster's hand. The monster howled as its hand was trapped by the door. Travis held the door down with the full weight of his body. The skin peeled off of the monster's hand as it dragged the appendage back into the column before the hatch door sealed shut and locked with a hiss.

Bang! Bang! Bang!

Travis fell back with a mixture of fear and relief and crab-walked himself over to the wall. He could feel the monster pressing on the door from beneath, but unlike the door to the locker room, there was no room for it to gain the leverage needed to bust the hatch open. *He hoped.*

A moment later the banging stopped. Travis collapsed in relief and took in his surroundings. The room was unfamiliar: Dozens of giant metal tanks surrounded the edge of the room. Pipes branched out from the tanks and either connected to other tanks or pipes or disappeared into the wall. Someone had scribbled on the tanks in multiple different languages, some he knew and others he didn't. Each tank bore the symbol for fire surrounded by an orange triangle. *This must be the exchange room and the tanks must be the different gasses that various species need to breathe.*

It occurred to him that he had no idea where this room was actually located within the outpost. Was he near the hangar? How far from the gate was he? As he stood, his head swum and his knees buckled.

He woke to find himself on the floor with a sore skull and damp pants. *When had he wet himself?* The thought made him want to laugh and, given everything that had happened, Travis didn't think anyone would fault him for wetting his pants for the first time since he was six.

He groaned, rolled onto his knees, and attempted to stand. Legs wobbling and body aching, he made it to his feet and stumbled to the door, ordered it open. Travis stalled in the threshold, horrified by what he saw. Outside the door, the walls and floor of the hallway were cracked and pitted. A long, red stain coated the floor in both directions. His heart rate accelerated, his head thumping to the tattoo of his heartbeat. He knew this hallway. To the left was the hangar and the Avealus Gate. To the right was the waiting area. He stepped back into the exchange room and locked the door.

"Well, I am close to the hangar," Travis told himself. "Not that it means much."

Was the Gate as destroyed as the hallway he'd seen? And if it was, was there anything he could do to fix it? *Candace was right.* Knowing what these things were and what they were capable of, should he still try to repair the gate? Did it even matter anymore now that Devon was gone? He paced the room, each step sending a thousand stabs of pain to every part of his body, and each stab a grim reminder of everything that had happened since he'd left the rec room. Could he just sit here and wait to die, though? It'd be easier to just open the hatch and let the monster finish what it had started, but something wouldn't let him.

He needed a plan, an objective. At most, they — no, he — needed to warn the other outposts, which meant fixing the gate enough to establish a network connection. But fudge, that would be dangerous. *Maybe too dangerous.* He needed to talk to Candace. The thought made him ache, because who he really needed in that moment was Devon, and Devon was —

"Travis?"

He shot away from the hatch expecting to see the monster climbing through, but it remained shut.

"You there, friend?" Candace asked. Travis slumped down in the corner of the room. "Where's Devon?"

"I'm here," he said with a dead voice, his hands pressed over his eyes. "Devon isn't. He's —" He couldn't finish the sentence, not even in his mind. The idea of it, the reality of it, was too much.

Candace's heavy breathing filled the room. "I am so sorry."

It sounded like she actually meant it.

"This isn't what I wanted," Candace said. "I just wanted to

keep you from getting to the gate. I just wanted to keep those things from getting to Vexel. You saw what they can do. I can't let them get out of our outpost. I had to do something. I never thought it would get you or Devon."

Travis heard the words but they slid off his mind like a fried egg off Teflon. All he could focus on was how she had sabotaged him from the very beginning.

I just wanted to keep you from getting to the gate.

I just wanted to keep you from getting to the gate.

I just wanted to keep you from getting to the gate.

The words repeated over and over in his mind. He understood them. They were plain words. Simple. They couldn't mean what they seemed to mean. Candace couldn't have — wouldn't have — let that thing out. The idea had never even occurred to him.

I never thought it would get you —

The door must have been blasted open during the explosion. Destroyed like the floors and walls not far from where he sat. Or maybe the monster had battered it down like the ones in the locker room.

— or Devon.

"Bitch." Travis scoffed, but it was more of a growl. Hate bubbled inside him like poison. All his fear, uncertainty, and pain burned away in the rage that boiled up from his gut and filled him like white hot light.

"What?"

CANDACE

Travis was quiet on the other end. Candace gazed across the hangar to the hall with the blasted door. He was right there. Down a short hallway, tucked away snuggly in a small room. So close. *Too close.* Not that it mattered. The monster would see to that. She heard it scuttling along the ceiling.

"I'm going to kill you," Travis said loudly. It struck her like a punch to the gut. "How could you? *Why* would you?"

"I —"

"You're supposed to be in charge. I was ready to agree with you. Work with you. But now? Fuck you."

"Trav —"

"No! Now I am going to do what Devon and I set out to do. I *am* going to get the gate working, and I *am* going to tell everyone what you did." His voice cracked as he shouted.

She could throw a hundred things at him in response: how Devon's death was more his fault than hers. That they should have stayed in the rec room. That they should have listened to her from the start. But they all rang false. No, not false. They stank of bullshit. Travis was right, and sorry wasn't good enough. But that didn't change the situation. She hadn't done a good thing, but she had done the *right* thing.

"It had to be done," she said to Travis. "That thing can't be let off-world. You can kill me if you want to. I won't even stop you. I fucked up, and I know it. This is all my fault. And it sucks that you all have to pay for my fuck up with your lives, but that is where we are at. So, get over it, because I'm not letting you get to the gate. I'm not gonna let you kill billions to spite me."

She stared out the window, silent, thinking. She thought about the twenty-five-year career she'd had and how it ironically was ending. She thought about the one hundred and ten people who died. About Devon. About Travis. But mostly, she thought about Julia. She was never going to see her wife again. Their last words to each other had been stupid and spiteful. What would Julia think when she heard? Or had she heard already? Would she still take their savings and buy that place on Traxis? The one on the lake? Or would she just stay put? All the thoughts of Julia almost made Candace want to get out of Travis's way and let him fix the gate so she could see Julia, hear her voice one last time.

Candace wanted to rip her own heart out. But it was a good hurt. It was important to maintain perspective. As badly as she needed to see Julia, she needed to protect her more. Travis wanted to save those who were still alive here, and nothing she said would change his mind. But what if there were no people to save?

That would be easy enough.

AEON

Aeon was done. Abso-fucking-lutely done. The door wouldn't open. He had tried using his own clip and let the others handle the wires, but when that hadn't worked, he'd been forced to try the wiring himself on someone else's clip. None of it worked. It was all Travis and Devon's fault. Nothing worked like it was supposed to. *They escaped and left us behind. Fuckers. I'm going to rip them apart. Beat their skulls against the walls.*

His stomach seized. The hunger cramps were deep now. They had water and booze, but nothing to eat. Soon they would start eating each other. A horrible thought now, but in a day or two probably less so. He would give anything — *anything* — for something to eat.

It would be better to just burn the door down, but as these idiots were so emphatic to point out that it wouldn't work. They would all just end up as cooked meat with no one to enjoy the meal.

"What are we gonna do?" Anna asked him. She looked terrible. Her red hair was limp and greasy, and the bags under her eyes made her face look like smooshed clay.

"I don't fucking know," he said bitterly. The sound of that

traitor Devon dying still rang in his ear. They couldn't escape that way, and if that creature — whatever it was — had managed to get into the locker room, what was to stop it from getting into the rec room?

How did I get here? Twenty years of work down the drain. Gone. And his race — the entire human race — was still dwindling. Fucking race traitors breeding with lesser species, or not breeding at all. Just fucking for the joy of it. Was there a greater sin than that? Now, there were more half-breeds than actual humans. Hell, Earth was the only pure human planet left.

But there had been nothing there for him. He expected to find more humans like him at Zurathel Transport Corp, those who feared the slow death of their people. But no one did. Now he was going to die on a backwater rock surrounded by half-breeds and traitors all because he'd dared to speak the truth. Fuckers. Had his superiors sent him here to silence him? Did they know this would happen? It seemed too much of a coincidence that right after he'd arrived that shit had hit the fan. *Go on Aeon, clean toilets, mop floors, and launder the sweat and cum stains from the sheets of faggots. You won't have to do it for long.*

No. It was not going to happen. He was going to get out of here and go home.

"You have to have some idea," Anna said. "You have to. This isn't right. They can't just forget about us."

"Well, they fucking did. So shut the fuck up and get away from me." He walked back through the crowd to the bar. That bitch Rita was sitting in the corner across the room with someone, their heads close together. He thought about walking over and ramming his knee into her face over and over until his knee popped out the back of her skull. No one would stop him. But he didn't. He wanted a drink more.

"Hello," Candace said. "Rec room if you can hear me, speak up."

Aeon turned around on the spot and marched towards the

mic box. The three who stood around it froze and turned to him for guidance.

The sight of silent obedience made him hard.

Six quick little strides and Aeon was there. When he grabbed the transmitter, he saw an extra attachment on the bottom, but filed it away for later.

"What?" he barked. Static hissed. "What the fuck do you want? Want to gloat more? Brag about killing us? What?"

Candace sighed. "I wanted to let you know that Travis got the gate working. We are fifteen minutes until alignment, so I've unsealed the door. Get here quick or get left behind."

The hair on Aeon's body stood on end. She, this cunt, was giving him orders. "Listen here —" he began, but he didn't think anyone heard him. Cheers had erupted all around him.

"Shut up!" Aeon ordered. Some listened, looking at him with frightened reserve, but he could see his control on them bleeding away.

"Don't you see?" he said to a crowd of cheering people. Then he saw Rita and her compatriot move through the throng of milling bodies, not walking toward the door with the group, but toward the back wall. What did they know?

He followed them.

RITA

ravis was right. Candace was leading them to slaughter. She thought about telling the others, and maybe a few would listen, but between Aeon's shouting and listening to the attack on Devon, there was no rational person left but her and Corin. As the masses surged to the door and waited for it to open, Rita and Corin moved to the far corner of the room.

"How can they be so stupid?" Corin asked. "If the gate was working, our clips would be working too."

Rita didn't answer him. Her attention was focused on Aeon. The big man was pushing against the flow of the crowd. Heading for her and Corin. The sight of him made her wish she could dissolve into the wall. Her body still ached from his last beating.

"What the fuck are you two doing back here," he yelled over the cacophony of voices.

"We aren't doing anything," Corin whispered. Rita had told him everything Travis had said. Now she wished she hadn't. He was a bad liar and a coward too.

"Bullshit. What are you two scheming about." Aeon puffed himself up.

Fuck it. "Travis warned us that this was a trap. He hasn't fixed the gate yet. There really is something out there. You heard it kill Devon."

Aeon's gaze bored into her. His eyes darted between her and Corin. It was like he was viewing a tennis match, waiting to see who the winner was before deciding if she was telling the truth or not. His features were more ape-like than ever.

"Is that your thing on the bottom of the box?" he asked.

Rita nodded.

"And who said you could do that?"

"No one," she said defiantly. "And I don't need anyone's permission. Least of all yours."

Aeon took a step toward her and placed his fist on her cheek. "Are you sure of that?"

Rita tried to swallow, to pull at the tiny ember of courage she'd been tending all day, but her throat seized, and the ember began to fade.

"Yes," Corin said. "Yes, we are. And you should be glad we did. We have to stop everyone from leaving. They are going to get killed out there."

"That's a lie, and you know it. There ain't nothing out there. Never was. Everything we heard down there below the hatch was a fucking act. And this," — he gestured to Rita and Corin — "this is the trap. I bet Candace knew we would get out on our own soon. She pretended to let us out, then got you two to say we needed to stay so we'd stop trying to escape on our own. Yeah. I bet that is it."

"It's not!" Rita shouted. "Please. Believe me. I don't want to be stuck here with you. You ugly, mean, stupid, piece of shit. But I don't want to see you die. Please. Tell them. They'll believe you. They won't believe us. You're in charge here. Tell them. Save them. Please."

Aeon glowered at her for a moment, then grinned. "Ugly, am I? Stupid. Mean. I wish I had the time to show you ugly. I could teach you a few things. Remind you what your role is to our kind." With that, he squeezed her stomach just above the pelvis. He leaned over and whispered in her ear. His hot breath spread like sewage against her face. "I have places to be. After I'm done saving everyone from that crazy cunt and your friends, I'll come back for you."

He huffed and walked back through the crowd. Rita let out a long breath. Then he stopped in his tracks. He turned back smiling. Every ounce of heat was blasted out of her body. It wasn't a smile at all. It was a leer.

He stomped back toward her.

"Actually," Aeon said, "I think it will be better if you come with me. If there is something out there, it'll be good to have someone to throw at it."

Rita screeched as Aeon grabbed her arm. She clawed and punched at the hand that held her as he dragged her out the door, but her blows might as well have been gusts of wind for all the good they did her.

TRAVIS

ravis had a plan. It was not a good plan. He would probably end up getting himself killed, and that was only if it worked. This was not a comforting thought, but Devon's death had robbed him of any desire to move on.

Sitting against the wall in the exchange room, sixty feet from his goal, Travis felt further from home than he had ever been. And why even go home? He'd been happier during his three years at this outpost than he had ever been in his entire life. What was waiting for him on Earth? Noise and smells of life and rot? He couldn't stay here. The image of that thing wearing Devon's face and speaking with his voice now covered every inch of this place like mildew on a shower wall.

Just get everyone out safely. Get them all home. They won't thank me, especially that creep Aeon, but it doesn't matter. In spite of what Candace said, of what she believed, there *was* a way to save everyone and keep that thing from escaping.

There had to be.

At least he had warned all of them in the rec room. They wouldn't fall for Candace's trap. At least he hoped not. Aeon may throw that all out the window, but all he had was hope, so hope would have to do.

Thinking of Aeon and worrying about Candace wasn't helping. He needed to work on his own plan. And pray he didn't die.

BELOW

I t skulked along the black grid beneath the outpost. The presence of the man above still enraged it. That something might block its way had never occurred to it. This was not something that happened. The material world should fall apart; it was *meant* to fall apart.

It stopped as the world began to vibrate — not far away but far enough that it only registered on the edges of its awareness. The meat was moving in a pack. The thing quickened its pace. It found the long metal spine it had descended earlier.

Flecks of light drifted down like falling snow

AEON

T he door opened. Clotted blood along the door jamb made an odd squealing noise that hung in the air and made Aeon's balls tighten.

The mob rushed past him into the empty hall. Rita thrashed and pulled at his grip like a fucking animal. Even the squeals she elicited were more pig-like than human. It was disgusting.

"Move," Aeon said, shoving her in front of him. Rita stumbled forward, shaking as she walked. Her head turned in every direction. She certainly was committed to the lie. Corin walked closely behind him.

The smell of piss and shit wafted after the others, tainting the sterility of the hallway.

They rounded the first corner to the sight of half a dozen bodies. Ten people from the crowd in the rec room stood around the corpses. Crying. Moaning. *Idiots. Do they think they can save people who have been dead for days?*

"Please," Rita whined, shrinking away from the bodies. Her eyes bulged, pleading with him to let her go. Maybe she truly believed some monster stalked the halls. The stench stung his eyes as he skirted around the reeking dead and their would-be saviors, dragging Rita along by her wrist. Beyond them, the corridor was empty. All the others had gone. They were losing time.

"We have to go faster," Aeon said.

"No," Rita begged. "I can't. I won't."

Aeon lashed out and grabbed her by the hair. She squeaked and squalled. Those who lingered over the dead turned to him.

"Hey, enough man," one of them shouted.

"Stay out of it. This bitch is working with the others. I'm not letting her out of my sight."

Something screeched nearby. Everyone looked for the source of the sound. The hallway was empty, but the effect was like ice water down the spine.

"Maybe you're right," one of the others stammered. "Maybe we should move."

"Glad someone has some sense." Aeon grunted. He didn't wait for any other affirmation. He gripped the bitch's hair harder and dragged her onward. At first, she struggled but the thing screeched again and she stopped resisting. Aeon let go of her and grinned when she didn't try to run away.

On and on they went, taking lefts and rights, moving so fast they were nearly running. The layout of Outpost 9106 was larger and more spread out than others he had worked at, and he feared he was on the verge of becoming lost. They shouldn't have paused back there and let the rest — the ones that knew the way — get ahead of them.

"Shit." Aeon skittered to a stop.

To his right, metal lockers lay crumpled in heaps through the hole in the wall. What the fuck had done that?

Click, click, click, click.

Ragged buzzing like static filled his mind. Something moved to his left. He could hear coarse, raspy breathing. A glance in that direction broke him. His bowels turned to liquid, his bladder tightened, his balls shriveled.

Something stood there wearing the face of Devon. Dull black holes sat where his eyes should have been.

Aeon turned to grab Rita, but was met with a wall of people staring murder at him. His hand went for her hair but missed as she dodged back. Three pairs of hands flew forward and slammed into his chest. Aeon stumbled backward into the open hallway towards the monster. He spared the monster a glance and then retreated back down the hall. He looked back just in time to see the others fleeing around a corner and out of sight.

"Why did none of you help me?" the monster demanded in Devon's voice.

Aeon needed to run. There were three ways he could go. Right to the ruined locker room and the tunnels beyond. Left to try to run past the monster. Or back the way he had come and hope to outrun the others.

Right, left, back. Where to go? What to do?

Back.

Aeon turned on numb legs and stumbled.

The monster lunged forward. Aeon spun and bolted after the others. The monster closed the forty-foot distance in seconds, skidded past the turn, halted and skittered after the man. Aeon could feel it closing in. His chest was on fire. His lungs pumped like bellows. At the first turn, he launched himself to the left. There was no sign of the others. Pushing himself as much as he could, he sprinted.

"Come back! It hurts! Make the pain stop!"

Five feet from the turn, something slammed into his back and Aeon was thrown into the wall. His skull struck first. *Crack.* Blood coated the side of his face.

Long sharp claws raked down his back, splitting flesh and muscle like they were paper. He was going to die.

Aeon tried to scream, but couldn't. He bit clean through his tongue and shattered his teeth. He clawed at the ground. Tried to crawl away. The monster stalked closer. Out of the corner of his eye, Aeon could see the skin-covered paw, with talons covered in gore.

The thing lifted its paw. Aeon wrestled himself onto his back to try and block the swipe. The creature tore his arm clean off. His scream of pain was nothing more than a gurgle, low and gravely. A nub of bone protruded from where the other half of his bicep had been. Blood gushed, coating his chest, the floor, and the monster itself. It shrieked in ecstasy. The weight of its joy pressed on Aeon's mind, mixing and melting with his terror, pain, and anguish until he could not tell one from the others. He began to revel in the emotions and find bliss in his demise.

Why am I not dead yet? The trauma to his skull, the loss of his arm, and so much blood, any one of those would have done him in. Yet nothing dimmed. His sight, his mind were as clear as ever.

The monster's claw ripped through the skin on the top of his head and glided along the skull, down the center of his face, his throat, and then his chest like it was pulling down a zipper.

CANDACE

Candace watched the monster tear Aeon to shreds. She thought she had understood. She thought . . . she thought . . . but she hadn't. Aeon thrashed wildly as the monster slit him open. Blood poured across his body. Then the monster began to peel him. It was almost gentle as it separated his skin from the skeleton beneath. Somehow, he seemed to remain conscious as his eyes danced wildly. His jaw opened and closed. She could see his half-tongue and broken teeth. Then the creature flipped him, and Aeon's thick insides flowed free of their cavity.

When it was done, the monster stepped into this new skin, adding it to its body. Giving it four new limbs and a second face.

Candace clicked to the feed of the other outpost crew making their way toward the hangar, far ahead of the monster.

She found herself reaching toward the control panel to seal the hangar door, to block the fleeing group from entering it. She couldn't do this, could she? Now that she understood, could she feed these people to the giant monster in the hangar?

Her hand hovered over the button. Two inches and she could save them. She could warn them to hide. To contact Travis and ask for his help. Beg for his help. If he listened, she might see Julia.

Julia. *Julia.*

Candace pulled her hand away and let it fall to her side. She couldn't chance it. The thing would escape from here with them.

"You don't know that," she said in Jackson's voice.

But I do.

Across the hangar, the Avealus Gate stood tall and whole, still missing the black on the inside, but ready to be activated.

AEON

Kill me. Please kill me. Please. Please. Please.

Every inch of Aeon's body was on fire. The monster crooned. The words it exclaimed were in his own voice. And Devon's. Aeon's eyes rolled, and the world rolled with it. His muscles twitched. He could feel the weight of his muscles and bones squishing his spongy insides. He tried to breathe but his lungs no longer worked. His mind yearned for air, or relief, or death but none came. *Why can't I die? Why won't it let me? Why does my suffocation fill me with exaltation?*

A shadow passed over him. The beast, the monster, the creature was leaving. First, he saw the heads, then the first paws — a mismatched set of a human arm and leg pulled like taffy, long and thin. Then the second set. The third set was still invisible yet he could feel it as it crushed his skull and brain. The pressure caused his eye to pop from its socket and spin out across the floor sending waves of vertigo across his disembodied mind as his vision spun in sync with the eye. Still Aeon lived.

He lived just long enough to watch the thing lumber around the corner and out of sight. Then the world faded. Drifting away in time with the monsters slowly receding footsteps.

TRAVIS

he comms clicked off when the conversation with Rita had ended. There was no time. Rita had told Travis that everyone had fled the refuge of the rec room headed to the gate. Travis needed to get it working before they got there. Moving was the hardest part of this. The cuts on Travis's blood-soaked leg spasmed every time that foot struck the floor. In the hall, the broken floor made speed impossible. Every step was painful and unstable. Weaving, stumbling, using the wall to hold himself up. Exhaustion set in as the adrenaline ebbed away. His mind was clouded. He recited his plan over and over in his head to keep the grief and fear at bay.

The tunnel turned and he could see the hangar. Wide open and utterly destroyed. It was like the long wave breakers at the lake he had visited as a child: Random blocks of stones piled together stretching out far into the water. Except, there was no water here, and the stone was stained brown with dried blood instead of black and green with muck.

He took three steps when something struck him from behind. Light exploded in his skull and he stumbled. Befuddled and confused he spun around expecting to see the monster ready to do to him what it had done to Devon.

Jared stood there, pipe in hand. His eyes were sunken in, deep purple shadows, blood and dirt smeared his cheeks and his suit was a tattered ruin. He looked half-dead. The pipe swung up and Travis raised an arm to block the second blow. It cracked into his forearm with a metallic snap sending him grunting to his knees.

"Why?" Travis groaned. "Why?"

Jared didn't speak, only stared at Travis with dead eyes and a mad grin. Travis cradled his broken arm against his chest, staring at the face of his demise. Jared reached out with a gloved hand and grabbed a fistful of Travis's hair and pulled him deeper into the hallway.

Travis was too bewildered to fight. He limped and stumbled as he walked bent over at the waist.

"Have you seen them yet?" Jared asked as they turned the corner. "Aren't they beautiful? I can feel them all the way through me. They are in my bones, my blood. That's why I have to stop you. I am they, and they are me. And when they leave here, I will go with them and live forever."

Jared tugged Travis forward and his grip on Travis's hair slipped. Travis stumbled backward and stood. Fresh adrenaline burned through him. Travis anticipated the blow this time and he lunged at Jared as the pipe whistled through the air. His shoulders slammed into the other man's chest. There was a wet crack as the two of them fell to the broken concrete.

Jared spat blood into Travis's face. Travis pushed himself quickly to his feet, wiping frantically at the fresh blood. Jared laughed and began to rock back and forth. The pipe grated against the stone. When he swiped it at Travis again, there was no strength to it. Travis grabbed the pipe with his good hand and pulled it free from Jared's grip. It was sticky with his blood.

Jared giggled. "I will stop you. I will, I will. I will stop you, and when they leave here I will go with them and live forever."

Jared sat up, and when he did, he left a large chunk of his

skull and his brains on the jagged stone. He laughed all the louder. Exultant. Jubilant. Relishing in the pain.

His eyes bulged and he groaned with pleasure. "Do you see now?"

Travis couldn't listen anymore. The sight of all that blood was less disgusting than the words.

"It killed Devon," Jared whispered. "It killed him and skinned him and now it's wearing him like clothes. Did you know that?"

Travis's head began to swim and buzz. The anger he kept pressed down, the grief and pain came boiling out.

"Did you?" Travis demanded.

"Yes. Of course. It must be done. It must."

Travis backhanded Jared with the pipe and struck his shoulder, sending him sprawling.

"Don't you understand?" Jared asked. Blood leaked from his mouth, nose, and ears.

Travis really looked at him then. The front of his suit was torn open, and there were deep punctures all over his bare chest. There was no reason he should be alive. It wasn't natural. It wasn't right. Why should Jared live when Devon had died? Devon, more than anyone here, had deserved to live through this. But that wasn't an option. Not anymore.

Now, the best Travis could do was help the others. He studied Jared. The hole in his head, his chest. Travis had to ensure the others escaped with their lives. Survived. He raised the pipe.

"Do what you will, but it won't change anything," Jared said with solemnity.

Travis swung the pipe. It swept across Jared's face breaking it open like a ripe melon Blood and teeth and skin flew. He pulled back and swung again. Jared's jaw tore loose. It dangled on a scrap of loose cheek.

Jared collapsed, but Travis didn't stop. He bashed once, twice, ten more times. When he was done, he and the hall were painted red. Fat droplets of blood swelled to the tips of his gloved fingers and plopped onto the floor with a splash. Nothing remained of Jared's grinning face.

Something caught Travis's eye as he turned away. A bulge in Jared's pocket. He bent down and pulled out a pack of cigarettes and a metal lighter. It had been years since he'd smoked. His mom told him they used to be made with plants. Now they were synthetic. "All Buzz, No Bad" was even printed on the bottom of the pack. He shoved the cigarettes and lighter into his pocket.

The feeling of being watched overwhelmed him. He turned sure he would find the monster watching him, but the hall was empty except for him. Was the monster invisible again? Or was there another one that had yet to find skin to wear. His eyes searched for anything to indicate where the attack would come from when they landed on spot a dozen feet away. The black eye of a camera stared blankly at him from its perch on the ceiling.

He flipped it off.

"Fuck you, Candace," Travis said and limped back toward the hangar dragging the bloody pipe across the jagged ground. He had a gate to fix.

RITA

ita shouted at the running crowd to stop, to follow her, to hide, but no one listened. Her voice was lost among the others, and she was dragged along with the tide of the fleeing crew.

The crowd surged around the last corner and stampeded their way down to the tall door that led to the Avealus Gate. The mass of bodies stopped, bottlenecked at the entrance. Too afraid to move forward, too stupid to run back. She searched for Corin, to ask him what had made them all stop, but he had weaseled too deep into the mix of others for her voice to reach him.

One by one they herded out into the hangar, louder than a pack of mewling animals. Rita watched, caught between curiosity and dread. Behind her was an intersection. The path to the left led to the control room and the path right would take her back into the maze of the outpost.

The gap between herself and the rest of the crowd widened as they filtered through the doorway. They spread slowly out into the cavernous hangar beyond. She saw a few of them stumble and trip. Their neighbors had to hold them up, but still they ambled forward.

"No!" someone screamed. "Run!"

She didn't know whose voice it was or why they were shouting, but she didn't need to. Before any of the people in front of her could begin to register what was happening, Rita turned right and sprinted deeper into the outpost. *At least I know what waits for me there.*

TRAVIS

"No!" Travis screamed. "Run!" He stood in his entrance to the hangar watching helplessly as the crew streamed through their doorway onto the killing floor.

He screamed and screamed and screamed but his voice could not reach across the nine-hundred feet to the crew pouring in on the other side of the hangar.

The massive thing descended on the crowd from above. Two fleshy arms gripped the cracked stone ceiling, stretching longer and longer like threads of spider webbing as it dropped, while its hundreds of other arms reached for the ground and its prey like tentacles. The slowly spreading crowd hadn't seen it. They were too transfixed by the destruction at their feet. Halfway down, the monster let go and dropped to the floor with a boom. A plume of dust billowed out and swept across the hangar. The shockwave knocked Travis into the wall and he choked on air that reeked of death and tasted of blood.

The monster reared up out of the dust cloud to tower over the assembled masses. It was almost the full height of the gate. Travis guessed it must be nearly five hundred feet long.

Through the haze, he could see the dim outline of the crowd frozen in the sudden quiet that followed the boom.

"Run goddammit!"

The sound of his scream seemed to break the hold the monster had on them and they scattered. Some running back the way they'd come, others making a break from the corridor where Travis stood.

The monster rejoiced.The chorus of a hundred different voices echoed throughout the hangar.

"Help me!"

"Save me!"

"Please! It hurts!"

The pain in their voices was more than Travis could handle. He turned and ran.

"Wait!"

"Don't leave us!"

Whether these were the cries of the living or dead Travis didn't know and he didn't look to see. He ran. Every part of his mind propelled him forward. Almost there. He fell, scrambled up and ran. The open doorway to the exchange room beckoned him on. Pleas of the dead and dying chased him as he ran, and only ceased when the door hissed shut behind him.

CANDACE

andace held her breath when the six-inch thick glass splintered and the thing came off the ceiling. *How many tons were there beneath the skin of all that dead?* Candace did her best to see what happened next.

Travis had fled the hangar. She couldn't blame him. Bearing witness was her penance for bringing this madness on them all. She deserved worse. She deserved to be down there with the others who were making payment for her mistake, but she couldn't let herself do it, not while Travis was still alive. After he was dead and there was no chance of the monster ever leaving, she would seek the monster out and let it have her too.

Even through the fractured and splintering glass, she could see the chaos in the hangar. Too many people had entered and they couldn't all get back through the door quickly enough. Thirty — or maybe forty — tried to fit through a door meant for two at the most. That would be their death sentence. Six of them understood this and charged across the hangar toward the waiting area. She prayed for them. As big as the monster was, it couldn't get them too, and so they at least stood a chance of escaping.

Candace's mouth dropped. Then the thing changed. It bent,

twisted, and stretched, its front half crawled towards the crowd bottlenecked at the door while its back half extended towards the six fleeing in the other direction.

Strands of human skin tore away like cable from a suspension bridge, breaking one after another. The sound of it stretching carried into the control room. It sounded like a high-tension wire being pulled taut. The keening noise grew. Time seemed to crawl and then . . . it was over.

There were two of them now, and Candace finally understood where the smaller one had come from.

Before she could give it any more thought, the front monster lunged at the tiny specs pushing to get through the small door.

While the front monster surged forward, the rear monster turned and charged at the six fleeing for the waiting area. They didn't even make it halfway across the hangar before it was upon them. One long sweep of an arm sent them scattering like broken toys. Then it began to flay them. One at a time.

More than half of those amassed at the entrance into the outpost had made it through the door before the monster reached them. Half a dozen hands grabbed, slashed, crushed, and squished the fifteen that hadn't gotten through, discarding the chunky bits that were left. When it was done, the monster pressed itself against the door and began to squeeze through. It shrunk and elongated. Like putty being pushed through a tube it changed its shape and form.

Candace followed the monster's progress on the monitors. It slinked like a snake after her crew. It crushed one after another, buckled walls and deformed the floor and ceiling as it moved.

Back in the hangar, the second monster finished skinning its six victims and then moved onto the others the first monster had left behind. It worked quickly, growing in size with each new skin it added to its body. When it was done, it sauntered over to the larger monster that was still squeezing itself through the hangar door. It reattached itself like two chunks of clay being smushed back together. Minutes later, the rest of it was gone. Vanished into the outpost.

Candace watched through the control room window as the victims mouthed their silent agony and thrashed on the craggy floor of the hangar. They pulled at their guts, trying to squish themselves back together. Or tried to drag themselves toward severed limbs until one by one, they went still then silent. It started with the victim furthest from the hangar door and then the next furthest, as if an invisible bubble of life drifted away, following closely behind the creature.

As the last person stopped moving, the hangar was silent again.

The sight of friends — people she had spent years getting to know and like — dying like that was too much for her. She flipped a series of switches on the console. The sound of scraping metal filled her ears as the air was sucked out of all of the open areas in the outpost. Candace hoped that this at least would lead to a more merciful death. It was all she could offer them. It was too bad it didn't work. There was no mercy in Outpost 9106. Not for her, not for her friends, not for anyone.

Death had been patient, but it wasn't going to be patient any longer.

TRAVIS

he sound of the oxygen exchanges kicking on next to him was deafening in the small room. It only took a moment for Travis to understand what that meant: Candace had finally decided to vent the atmosphere out of the outpost again. *Gods damn her.* He scrambled to put on his suit helmet before rushing across the room to pick up the roll of black gaffer tape there. Air hissed out as he wrapped tape around his leg to seal the blood-stained gashes in the suit.

Travis waited to feel the pull as the air in his room was sucked out. Prepared himself for the silence that would follow. His breath fogged the plastic of his helmet. But the pull never came. The air in his room hadn't vented.

Travis took a long steadying breath to calm his panic. Only then did he realize what Candace's actions might do to his plan. What it might change. He stood and began a slow inspection of the enormous exchange tanks. All of his additions to the pipes and valves were as he had left them. And the sudden venting hadn't caused any of the tanks to rupture. When his inspection was done, he pulled up the directory on his clip and stared at the command prompts he had established. They were ready and waiting for him. Engineering may be his background, but he had never constructed a bomb before, and he hoped that he would never need to again. But he thought it would work. Prayed it would work.

Travis limped back over to the wall and took off his helmet and pulled out one of the cigarettes and tried to light it with his good hand, but it shook too much. He steadied his arm with the wall in order to get the flame to the tip of the cigarette. It tasted like actual peaches, but burned his mouth and throat when he inhaled. He choked and sputtered. The chemicals hit his blood like lightning and his head like a hammer, but the pain in his body faded a shade, and it became bearable to walk.

He had to fix the gate. That hadn't changed. Nothing had changed. Not really. And once that was done, he could pop the tanks and blow this whole place back to the Gods. How long would it take for the outpost to fill with the unmixed flammable gas and for the pressure in the back flow tanks he'd rigged to go critical and to blow? Long enough. But first the gate. He pulled the helmet back over his head and twisted the seals. The air that flooded in tasted sterile and metallic.

Travis left the room. He avoided looking at Jared's body as he walked back down the hall towards the hangar. Or at least tried to. It was impossible though. His blood was everywhere. What was left of the man was splayed out in the center of the hall. He skirted past the pulpy remains of Jared's skull and stepped over the splayed limbs of his corpse.

At the end of the corridor he stopped. Hugging the wall, he peeked around the fractured corner of the hall doorway and out into the hangar. Bile shot up his throat as he took in the massacre. He swallowed it back down and returned to his survey of the scene. His path seemed clear. The monster must still be in the halls chasing after the other survivors.

The thought pulled Travis up short. His hand went absently to the flimsy plastic hood over his head, before looking up to the control room for the first time. Two hundred feet off the ground with large windows, it stood out like a grease mark on a white sheet. The glass may be spiderwebbed and marred and stained, but it was still whole. Candace was there. He could faintly see her, even from the other side of the hangar. She was motionless as she watched him.

"Nothing more you can do to me," he said to her over the comms channel, and then began to limp over the fractured concrete ground toward the gate. "I win."

Step by stumbling step Travis meandered his way to the gate. Even using the wall to steady himself, it took him longer than he liked. Candace couldn't do anything to him anymore, but that didn't mean the monster wouldn't return. In truth he knew it would eventually, and he needed to be done and gone by then.

Then he was there, standing beneath the ancient stone monolith like an ant beneath a full-grown oak. Standing close to the Avealus Gate, he could see that the damage done to it had healed, but the ever-present black was gone from within the center of the arch. He puzzled over it for a moment. When he touched the stone, he could not feel the hum of power that had always been there before. Then he knew what must be done to make it work. Assuming the mechanisms hadn't been destroyed in the explosion. If they had, then Candace would get her wish, and he would die here with her.

RITA

Rita ran, chest burning, through the open door to one of the living quarters.

"Bitch," she shouted as the door to one of the living quarters slammed shut behind her. Her shoulder clicked audibly in its socket and throbbed from slamming into the far wall.

That bitch Candace vented the air. "I need to get the fuck out of here." But she didn't know where to go. Those monsters were still in the hallways. There was no way to get to the locker room. The hangar wouldn't help her and she couldn't stay where she was. Eventually the monster would realize where she was and come for her. So what did that leave?

"I guess I could go and see Candace," she said with a laugh. "She'll probably kill me. But she won't get the jump on me, at least."

How far was it to the control room? Could she make it there with no breath in her lungs? Even if she ran as fast as she could, Rita didn't think so. What other choice did she have, though? It was the best out of an ocean of bad options. The only one.

CANDACE

andace watched impotently as Travis slammed the door of the breaker box shut. It had only taken him eight minutes to doom billions of lives. The instant he had thrown the last switch, the shimmering black inside the gate popped back into existence and the net went live. Like the signal had just been waiting quietly for its chance to reach across billions of lightyears to the relay here.

That was it.

They had lost.

Nothing Candace did now could undo what Travis had done. There were no controls to shut down the gate in the control room. Deadlocking the gate could delay the monster's escape, but it couldn't prevent it forever. If the Empire knew that creatures like this existed, why hadn't they created a way to shut the gates down permanently the way the explosion had? Her mind was gutted. Her heart was empty. She wanted to hate Travis. There was no one left to save but himself, and he knew the danger, even better than she did. They had both lost something, *someone*, but they were different forms of loss. At least the person she had lost was still alive and could go on living. Travis didn't have that. His loss was here. So while she understood why he did what he did, she didn't agree.

She wanted to thank Travis, though. Now at least, she had a chance to send Julia a goodbye.

TRAVIS

The entrance back into the main body of the outpost was a black spot. A cracked and heavily-dilated hole in the universe. Travis stepped into it without pausing. The monster had obliterated the corridor beyond it, destroying lights, scouring and bowing every surface outward like an ant tunneling through dirt. He could follow its path along the grid of the outpost by checking where the lights were gone and where they still glowed. Only a faint glimmer showed from the first branch to the right. All the rest was shadow. What waited for him there, he didn't know, and he no longer cared.

He hobbled on. Step, shuffle, step, shuffle. His injured leg could barely hold any weight, and the pipe he dragged along with him pulled painfully on his shoulder. His entire body was covered in a thick layer of sweat, and yet he shivered like it was just above freezing.

Every few steps, his vision drifted out along the edges. He could feel the blood pooling in his shoe, leaving the sock heavy and sodden.

"I'm coming," he mumbled. "For you Devon. I love you. I love you I love you I love you."

How he got to the correct turn and then the stairs leading up to the control room he didn't know. He sensed someone coming up behind him halfway up the stairs, but didn't bother to check. *Forward*. He needed all his focus just to make it the last few steps. *Climb*.

The metal door was shut. A single light hung over it, illuminating the muddled gray steel. It opened before he reached it. Without his command. The sudden blast of wind as the air escaped the pressurized room into the vacuum of the stairwell nearly knocked him down the stairs. If he had fallen, he would never have gotten back up. That was assuming he somehow managed to survive the fall.

Minutes later he was through the door and into the sudden brightness of the control room.

"Candace! Bitch!" Travis shouted over the gushing sound of the wind. She stood with her back to him and didn't move at the sound of her name.

Travis trudged a few steps closer to her. That was when he saw the small camera hovering in front of her face.

Candace turned to face him. Tears had left tracks through the blood and grime on her face. "Hi, Travis," she said. "Ready to finish this?"

He waited for the sight of her grief to make any impact on him. He had expected it, anticipated having to solidify his resolve against it, but the sight of her changed nothing in him. Travis no longer saw a woman, a person, or a friend. All he saw was the monster wearing Devon's face pleading for help, and the one who was responsible for making that happen.

Travis took a step closer to her and raised the pipe.

"Don't," someone shouted. Travis swiveled his head and found Rita panting in the door. Bruised, bloody, and covered in dirt, she looked as bad as he felt. How had he not heard her enter?

"She killed Devon," Travis said calmly. "She killed everyone, and she did it on purpose. All of this is her fault, and I am not going to let her rot comfortably in prison somewhere. I'm just not."

"You're right," Candace said. She smiled. "I should have shut down the gate when I felt the first vibrations before the transmission. Jackson wanted to. But I didn't let him. All I could think of was getting home. Getting back to Julia. I didn't want to blow my retirement, risk my marriage, piss all of you off by delaying our leave over what I thought would be nothing."

She took a breath and went on. "Once I knew what I had done, once I saw those things. I knew we were all dead. The only thing left was to decide how and when. I tried to spare everyone from those things. I thought it was better to die of starvation. I wanted to ask for your input, but it was so long before we got comms working. I had to make a choice. And when comms started again and I heard all of the commotion in the rec room, I couldn't tell everyone what was really going on. No one would have seen reason. You all proved that. You're proving that now."

Candace paused and met his eyes. "You know what that thing is. The explosion didn't even hurt it. You've seen what it does and what it's capable of. It doesn't eat the people that it kills. I don't even think it gets hungry. It just kills and grows. If it ever got loose on a planet like Vexel, it would mean billions of dead and we *can't* let that happen. Yet you're still giving it a way out of here."

Rita was silent. Travis waited to see if she would say anything. When she didn't, he raised the pipe.

"Don't, Travis," Rita whispered. "You can't just murder her. It's wrong. We can just leave her here. Tie her up and leave her."

Travis swung the pipe into the side of Candace's skull. Her body smacked the ground with a *thwump* and rolled. Red poured from the open wound, but he could see the rhythmic rise and fall of her chest. She looked at him when he stepped closer.

"I set the atmospheric tanks to blow up," he said. "And when the net came online, I made sure to send all of the recordings and documentation to command. Everyone knows what happened here. They are ready. And when I leave here, the outpost will explode. That may not kill the things but it will put the gate back into lockdown, and since no one will ever be able to get here, it will never come back online."

He leaned forward and nearly collapsed but Rita moved to him and held him steady. "Do you know what that means? Bitch."

Candace did her best to nod. Fresh tears splashed down her cheeks.

"That's right. If you had listened to me, worked with me, everyone could have lived. But you were so preoccupied with being in charge that you never even considered there was a better way. Devon died. You murdered him, set that thing on him, all for nothing." He spat. A thick glob of red tinged saliva landed on her cheek mixing with her drying tears.

He stood up straight, not happy with how much help he needed from Rita to do it, and hefted the pipe.

"Come on," Rita said, trying to pull him away. "You don't have to. Let's just go."

"No. I will never sleep another night if I don't." He raised the pipe and Rita took a step away sobbing silently. The air blasted out the open door. The vents hummed, letting fresh air into the room to compensate. But all Travis could hear was the hammering of his own heart. All he could feel was the rightness of the pipe in his hands.

"You were right," Candace moaned painfully. "But that doesn't make me wrong. Just because your plan worked, doesn't mean it was worth the risk. It could have all gone wrong. It still could. You know that. Don't forget it."

Travis swung it down, aiming for her head but missed and struck her chest. She screamed as the metal shattered her ribs. The next blow struck her shoulder. More screaming. The third blow found its mark and buried itself an inch deep in her head. Candace twitched a few times then went still.

When the body was done spasming, Travis let go of the pipe. It fell with a clang.

Travis didn't wait any longer. The clock in his clip told them they only had five minutes until the next alignment. He used the clip to turn the atmosphere in the outpost back on. It wasn't necessary for his plan, but Rita didn't have a suit and needed to breathe if she was going to make it to the gate. A second later, the room calmed and became quiet.

When he turned to Rita, she flinched away from him. He pulled off the hood, and the cool air assaulted his face. His vision swam and he finally did collapse as he tried to pull the rest of the suit off. He didn't have the strength to do it.

"Help me," he moaned.

TRAVIS

The journey back to the Avealus Gate was quicker than the one to Candace. Travis attributed this to Rita, who practically carried him. Now that the vacuum was no more, Travis could hear the voices of nearly two hundred people closing in on them. Every second those voices drew closer. There were only two minutes left until the gate aligned. Two minutes to stand in the open and wait. Wait and pray the monster didn't reach them. While they walked, the halls and tunnels were being flooded by the pure gasses that made up the atmosphere they breathed. Unlike the latter, they were not mixed and inert.

Travis had set the first part of his plan in motion while Rita had pulled the suit off his bloody and swollen body. As a doctor, she had hissed and fussed at the state of his wounds but didn't have the time to tend to them. Now they only had seconds left to wait. Travis pulled up the menu on his clip to overclock the other tanks. It would only take moments for the pressure to build, and when it did, they would pop like balloons, and the whole place would blow away like dandelion fluff.

In the video feed on his clip, Travis watched as the monster closed in. He was wrong. It didn't tunnel like an ant but a worm. He didn't need the clip any longer. He could see the monster through the ruined doorway. It seethed and squirmed. Thrashing like an angry python.

The female voice chirped through the comm system and began her countdown. Just thirty seconds.

The monster broke off chunks of the wall around the doorway in its furious struggle. Travis pulled up the prompt to begin to fill the atmospheric overflow tanks and clicked it. It was done. The tank's pressure would be building rapidly with every second.

Ten seconds. Nine. Eight. The monster stretched more. The part of its body in the hangar trying to rip itself free of the rest. The keening of its transformation as it worked to tear itself apart, the hum of its power, the maddening buzz hammering against their brains.

Four. Three. Two.

Strands of flesh snapped. The smaller monster struggled free. A pop so loud it ruptured his eardrums, echoed out. The world lurched. The floor tore apart in a gout of flames. Rita pulled him backward. For 1.2 seconds he was nowhere but Travis didn't notice. A million light years away, he fell onto Rita. Surrounded by armed men. A pristine black wall behind them, unblemished, unmoving, surrounded by an unharmed gate. Travis shut his eyes and let relief and grief wash over him, but a part of him waited. Waited to see if his plan had worked. He didn't even notice the hundreds of voices shouting orders at him in languages he didn't know, and he didn't care. Translations of their words flashed along the HUD of his clip but he didn't read them. Whatever happened next would happen, and it wouldn't be for him to deal with.

ABOUT LAWRENCE J. WEST

Lawrence J. West grew up on horror, science fiction, and fantasy stories. He was exposed to them early (his mother read him Stephen King's IT when was 5) and this has influenced every aspect of his life. After reading Dr Jekyl and Mr Hyde at the age of 7 he decided he wanted to be an inventor when he grew up. He would design flying cars, and fancy versions of computers, but as he grew up he began to attach stories to these inventions, create worlds inspired by Blade Runner, Alien, and even The Lord of the Rings to go along with them, and eventually the love for world building and storytelling won out over his love of mathematics and science (though these never went away).

To call him a nerd or a geek would be an understatement. He enjoys video games (primarily RPG's), anime, manga, reading, LARPing, and so much more. He has even begun collecting and playing Warhammer 40k. Many of these passions are things he shares with his wife and partners, and is working to pass them along to his son too. Lawrence is also very active in both the LGBTQIA+ and Polyamory communities in his local area.

ACKNOWLEDGMENTS

I can't believe I'm writing this as my first book is being prepared to be published! It started in 2019, and over the past four years my friends and family have helped push me across the finish line. I need to thank my friend, editor, and publisher Dakota Rayne, to my friend Stefanie Contreras who gave me much needed feedback when I was stuck during the editing process, and to all my friends and fellow writers who never ceased to encourage me to push on and keep going: Alexis Carroll, Amanda Stockton, Jae Vel, and Jonathan Mette this book wouldn't be coming out without you.

Last but never least, I dedicate this to my son. Silas, it's never early or too late to dream and dream big.

PLEASE LEAVE A REVIEW

Thank you for reading *Breached* by Lawrence J West!

We encourage you to review this book on our site and/or on Goodreads. As a small publisher, every review counts! We thank you for purchasing this book and hope you enjoy *Breached* and other books from Inked in Gray Press.

Keep up to date on our upcoming projects by signing up to our newsletter or checking out our website! We promise not to spam you or sell your information, though we will email you with store discounts and updates from our authors!

Kindest Regards,
The Inked Team